Praise for
BRIAN JACQUES'S novels of REDWALL

"Astonishing." —*Kirkus Reviews*

"Rousing adventure." —*Publishers Weekly*

"Old-fashioned swashbuckling adventure." —*Locus*

"Swashbuckling adventures told with great gusto in rousing words." —*Chicago Tribune*

"Brian Jacques has the true fantasy writer's ability to create a wholly new and believable world."
—*School Library Journal*

"Jacques extols the virtues of honor and valor ... [The Redwall novels] are a good read, with enticing maps, plenty of songs, a dose of natural history, and loads of excitement, charm and humor." —*The Irish Times*

continued ...

Redwall

The book that inspired a legend—the first novel in the bestselling saga of Redwall! The epic story of a bumbling young mouse who rises up, fights back . . . and becomes a legend himself . . .

"Reminiscent of *Watership Down* . . . *Redwall* is a thrilling tale of danger and adventure . . . an edge-of-the-seat, can't-put-it-down book with potential for classic status."
—*Parent's Choice*

Mossflower

Brave mouse Martin and quick-talking mousethief Gonff unite to end the tyrannical reign of Tsarmina—who has set out to rule all of Mossflower Woods with an iron paw . . .

"Packed with action and imbued with warmth . . . richly inventive."
—*Kirkus Reviews*

"Children are privileged to enter the rich world of Redwall and Mossflower. So are the parents who get to come along."
—*The Boston Phoenix*

Mattimeo

Slagar the fox embarks on a terrible quest for vengeance against the fearless mouse warrior Matthias, cunningly stealing away what he most cherishes: his headstrong son Mattimeo . . .

"A heroic adventure . . . splendid."
—Lloyd Alexander, Newbery Medal winner

"Jacques's realistically drawn characters are full of personality."
—*Publishers Weekly*

Mariel of Redwall

After she and her father were tossed overboard by pirates, the mousemaid Mariel seeks revenge against searat Gabool the Wild ...

"Astonishing stuff ... a satisfying ripsnorter of an adventure." *—Kirkus Reviews*

"A female protagonist and a touching reunion between father and daughter lend a contemporary touch to the series' well-established tradition of perilous battles and rousing adventure." *—Publishers Weekly*

Salamandastron

When the mountain stronghold of Salamandastron comes under attack, only the bold badger lord Urthstripe stands able to protect the creatures of Redwall ...

"A good yarn ... grand climax ... Jacques charms readers ... another winner." *—Booklist*

"Swashbuckling adventures told with great gusto in rousing words." *—Chicago Tribune*

Martin the Warrior

The triumphant saga of a young mouse destined to become Redwall's most glorious hero ...

"Wonderfully imaginative." *—New York Times Book Review*

"Readers will rejoice." *—Los Angeles Times*

continued ...

The Bellmaker

The epic quest of Joseph the Bellmaker to join his daughter, Mariel the Warriormouse, in a heroic battle against a vicious Foxwolf ...

"Filled with rousing adventure, strong characters, and vibrant settings." —*Boston Sunday Globe*

"Jacques spins another irresistible tale." —*Booklist*

Outcast of Redwall

The abandoned son of a ferret warlord must choose his destiny beyond the walls of Redwall Abbey ...

"Grand exploits ... another rousing saga." —*Booklist*

"Strongly plotted and spiced with a variety of secondary characters." —*Publishers Weekly*

Pearls of Lutra

A young hedgehog maid sets out to solve the riddle of the missing pearls of legend—and faces an evil emperor and his reptilian warriors ...

"Plenty of adventure." —*Publishers Weekly*

"The Redwall books ... add a touch of chivalry and adventure reminiscent of the King Arthur stories." —*The Arkansas Democrat Gazette*

The Long Patrol

The Long Patrol unit of perilous hares is called out to draw off the murderous Rapscallion army—in one of the most ferocious battles Redwall has ever faced . . .

"A feast for the faithful."   —*Publishers Weekly*

"A welcome episode for the series' legion of fans."
—*Booklist*

Marlfox

Two brave children of warrior squirrels embark upon a quest to recover Redwall's most priceless treasure from the villainous Marlfoxes . . .

"A richly imagined world in which bloody battles vie for attention with copious feasting and tender romancing."
—*The Cincinnati Enquirer*

"A grand adventure story. Once the reader is hooked, there is no peace until the final page."   —*Chicago Sun-Times*

The Legend of Luke

Martin the Warrior journeys to his homeland to learn about his father's legendary battle against a pirate fox . . .

"The Medieval world of Redwall Abbey—where gallant mouse warriors triumph over evil invaders—has truly become the stuff of legend."   —*Seattle Post-Intelligencer*

Also by Brian Jacques

REDWALL

MOSSFLOWER

MATTIMEO

MARIEL OF REDWALL

SALAMANDASTRON

MARTIN THE WARRIOR

THE BELLMAKER

SEVEN STRANGE AND DEADLY TALES

OUTCAST OF REDWALL

PEARLS OF LUTRA

THE LONG PATROL

MARLFOX

THE LEGEND OF LUKE

WELCOME TO REDWALL

Excerpts from

REDWALL

MARTIN THE WARRIOR

MATTIMEO

and

MARIEL OF REDWALL

by

Brian Jacques

ACE BOOKS, NEW YORK

WELCOME TO REDWALL

An Ace Book / published by arrangement with:
Redwall: the author
Martin the Warrior: Huchinson Children's Books, Random House UK, Ltd.
Mattimeo: Century Huchinson Ltd.
Mariel of Redwall: Huchinson Children's Books

PRINTING HISTORY
Redwall: Philomel Books hardcover edition / 1986
Ace mass-market edition / June 1998
Martin the Warrior: Philomel Books edition / March 1994
Ace mass-market edition / April 1995
Mattimeo: Huchinson Children's Books Ltd. edition / 1989
Philomel Books hardcover edition / 1990
Ace mass-market edition / February 1999
Mariel of Redwall: Huchinson Children's Books edition / 1991
Philomel hardcover edition 1992
Ace mass-market edition / March 2000
Welcome to Redwall / August 2000

The Penguin Putnam Inc. World Wide Web site address is
http://www.penguinputnam.com

Check out the ACE Science Fiction & Fantasy newsletter
and much more on the Internet at Club PPI!

ISBN: 0-441-00818-6

ACE®
Ace Books are published by The Berkley Publishing Group, a division of Penguin Putnam Inc., 375 Hudson Street, New York, New York 10014. ACE and the ''A'' design are trademarks belonging to Penguin Putnam Inc.

PRINTED IN THE UNITED STATES OF AMERICA

10 9 8 7 6 5 4 3 2 1

Redwall

Peaceful Redwall Abbey is threatened by the dreaded Cluny, a fierce one-eyed rat who has vowed to conquer the Abbey. But a brave young apprentice named Matthias will rise up and fight back!

CHAPTER

I

Matthias cut a comical little figure as he wobbled his way along the cloisters, with his large sandals flip-flopping and his tail peeping from beneath the baggy folds of an oversized novice's habit. He paused to gaze upwards at the cloudless blue sky and tripped over the enormous sandals. Hazelnuts scattered out upon the grass from the rush basket he was carrying. Unable to stop, he went tumbling cowl over tail.

Bump!

The young mouse squeaked in dismay. He rubbed tenderly at his damp snub nose while slowly taking stock of where he had landed: directly at the feet of Abbot Mortimer!

Immediately Matthias scrambled about on all fours, hastily trying to stuff nuts back into the basket as he muttered clumsy apologies, avoiding the stern gaze of his elder.

"Er, sorry, Father Abbot. I tripped, y'see. Trod on my Abbot, Father Habit. Oh dear, I mean. . . ."

The Father Abbot blinked solemnly over the top of his glasses. Matthias again. What a young buffoon of a mouse. Only the other day he had singed old Brother Methuselah's whiskers while lighting candles.

The elder's stern expression softened. He watched the little novice rolling about on the grass, grappling with large armfuls of the smooth hazelnuts which constantly seemed to escape his grasp. Shaking his old grey head, yet trying to hide a smile, Abbot Mortimer bent and helped to gather up the fallen nuts.

"Oh Matthias, Matthias, my son," he said wearily. "When will you learn to take life a little slower, to walk with dignity and humility? How can you ever hope to be accepted as a mouse of Redwall, when you are always dashing about grinning from whisker to tail like a mad rabbit?''

Matthias tossed the last of the hazelnuts into the basket and stood awkwardly shuffling his large sandals in the grass. How could he say aloud what was in his heart?

The Abbot put his paw around the young mouse's shoulder, sensing his secret yearnings, for he had ruled Redwall wisely over a great number of years and gained much experience of mouselife. He smiled down at his young charge and spoke kindly to him. ''Come with me, Matthias. It is time we talked together.''

A curious thrush perching in a gnarled pear tree watched the two figures make their way at a sedate pace in the direction of Great Hall, one clad in the dark greeny-brown of the order, the other garbed in the lighter green of a novice. They conversed earnestly in low tones. Thinking what a clever bird he was, the thrush swooped down on the basket that had been left behind. Twisters! The basket contained only hard nuts, locked tight within their shells. Feigning lack of interest, lest any other birds had been witness to his silly mistake, he began whistling jauntily a few bars of his melodious summer song, strolling nonchalantly over to the cloister walls in search of snails.

It was cool inside Great Hall. Sunlight flooded down in slanting rainbow-hued shafts from the high, narrow stained-glass windows. A million colored dust-motes danced and swirled as the two mice trod the ancient stone floor. The Father Abbot halted in front of the wall on which hung a long tapestry. This was the pride and joy of Redwall. The oldest part had been woven by the Founders of the Abbey, but each successive generation had added to it; thus the tapestry was not only a priceless treasure, it was also a magnificent chronicle of early Redwall history.

The Abbot studied the wonderment in Matthias's eyes as he asked him a question, the answer to which the wise mouse already knew. ''What are you looking at, my son?''

Matthias pointed to the figure woven into the tapestry. It was a heroic-looking mouse with a fearless smile on his handsome face. Clad in armor, he leaned casually on an impressive sword, while behind him foxes, wildcats and vermin fled in terror. The young mouse gazed in admiration.

"Oh, Father Abbot," he sighed. "If only I could be like Martin the Warrior. He was the bravest, most courageous mouse that ever lived!"

The Abbot sat down slowly on the cool stone floor, resting his back against the wall.

"Listen to what I say, Matthias. You have been like a son to me, ever since you first came to our gates as an orphaned woodland mouse, begging to be taken in. Come, sit by me and I will try to explain to you what our Order is all about.

"We are mice of peace. Oh, I know that Martin was a warrior mouse, but those were wild days when strength was needed. The strength of a champion such as Martin. He arrived here in the deep winter when the Founders were under attack from many foxes, vermin and a great wildcat. So fierce a fighter was Martin that he faced the enemy single-pawed, driving them mercilessly, far from Mossflower. During the rout Martin fought a great battle against overwhelming odds. He emerged victorious after slaying the wildcat with his ancient sword, which became famous throughout the land. But in the last bloody combat Martin was seriously wounded. He lay injured in the snow until the mice found him. They brought him back to the Abbey and cared for his hurts until he regained his strength.

"Then something seemed to come over him. He was transformed by what could only be called a mouse miracle. Martin forsook the way of the warrior and hung up his sword.

"That was when our Order found its true vocation. All the mice took a solemn vow never to harm another living creature, unless it was an enemy that sought to harm our Order by violence. They vowed to heal the sick, care for the injured, and give aid to the wretched and impoverished. So was it written, and so has it been through all the ages of mousekind since.

"Today, we are a deeply honored and highly respected Society. Anywhere we go, even far beyond Mossflower, we are treated with courtesy by all creatures. Even predators will not harm a mouse who wears the habit of our Order. They know he or she is one who will heal and give aid. It is an unwritten law that Redwall mice can go anywhere, through any territory, and pass unharmed. At all times we must live up to this. It is our way, our very life."

As the Abbot spoke, so his voice increased in volume and solemnity. Matthias sat under his stern gaze, completely humbled. Abbot Mortimer stood and put a wrinkled old paw lightly on the small head, right between the velvety ears, now drooping with shame.

Once more the Abbot's heart softened towards the little mouse. "Poor Matthias, alas for your ambitions. The day of the warrior is gone, my son. We live in peaceful times, thank heaven, and you need only think of obeying me, your Abbot, and doing as you are bidden. In time to come, when I am long gone to my rest, you will think back to this day and bless my memory, for then you will be a true member of Redwall. Come now, my young friend, cheer up; it is the Summer of the Late Rose. There are many, many days of warm sun ahead of us. Go back and get your basket of hazelnuts. Tonight we have a great feast to celebrate—my Golden Jubilee as Abbot. When you've taken the nuts to the kitchen, I have a special task for you. Yes indeed, I'll need some fine fish for the table. Get your rod and line. Tell Brother Alf that he is to take you fishing in the small boat. That's what young mice like doing, isn't it? Who knows, you may land a fine trout or some sticklebacks! Run along now, young one."

Happiness filled Matthias from tail to whiskers as he bobbed a quick bow to his superior and shuffled off. Smiling benignly, the Abbot watched him go. Little rascal, he must have a word with the Almoner, to see if some sandals could be found that were the right fit for Matthias. Small wonder the poor mouse kept tripping up!

CHAPTER

2

The high, warm sun shone down on Cluny the Scourge.

Cluny was coming!

He was big, and tough; an evil rat with ragged fur and curved, jagged teeth. He wore a black eyepatch; his eye had been torn out in battle with a pike.

Cluny had lost an eye.

The pike had lost its life!

Some said that Cluny was a Portuguese rat. Others said he came from the jungles far across the wide oceans. Nobody knew for sure.

Cluny was a bilge rat; the biggest, most savage rodent that ever jumped from ship to shore. He was black, with grey and pink scars all over his huge sleek body, from the tip of his wet nose, up past his green and yellow slitted eye, across both his mean tattered ears, down the length of his heavy vermin-ridden back to the enormous whiplike tail which had earned him his title: Cluny the Scourge!

Now he rode on the back of the hay wagon with his five hundred followers, a mighty army of rats: sewer rats, tavern rats, water rats, dockside rats. Cluny's army—fearing, yet following him. Redtooth, his second-in-command, carried a long pole. This was Cluny's personal standard. The skull of a ferret was fixed at its top. Cluny had killed the ferret. He feared no living thing.

Wild-eyed, with the terror of rat smell in its nostrils, the horse plunged ahead without any driver. Where the hay cart was taking him was of little concern to Cluny. Straight on the panicked horse galloped, past the milestone lodged in the earth at the roadside, heedless of the letters graven in the stone: "Redwall Abbey, fifteen miles."

Cluny spat over the edge of the cart at two young rabbits playing in a field. Tasty little things; a pity the cart hadn't stopped yet, he thought. The high warm sun shone down on Cluny the Scourge.

Cluny was a God of War!

Cluny was coming nearer!

CHAPTER

3

Beneath the Great Hall of Redwall, candles burned bright in their sconces. This was the Cavern Hole of the mice.

What a night it was going to be!

Between them, Matthias and Brother Alf had caught and landed a fully-grown grayling. They had fought and played the big fish for nearly two hours, finally wading into the shallows and dragging it to the bank. It was nearly two pounds in weight, a tribute to Brother Alf's angling skills combined with the youthful muscles of Matthias and their joint enthusiasm.

Constance the badger had to be called. Gripping the fish in her strong jaws, she followed the two mice to the Abbey kitchen and delivered the catch for them. Then she made her farewells; they would see her at the Jubilee feast that evening, along with many other Mossflower residents who had been invited to share the festivities.

Brother Alf and Matthias stood proudly beside their catch amid the culinary hustle and bustle until they were noticed by Friar Hugo. Busy as he was, the enormously fat Hugo (who would have no other title but that of Friar) stopped what he was doing. Wiping the perspiration from his brow with a dandelion that he held with his tail, he waddled about inspecting the fish.

"Hmm, nice shiny scales, bright eyes, beautifully fresh." Friar Hugo smiled so joyfully that his face disappeared amid deep dimples. He shook Alf by the paw and clapped Matthias heartily on the back as he called out between chuckles, "Bring the white gooseberry wine! Fetch me some rosemary, thyme, beechnuts and honey, quickly. And now, friends, now,'' he squeaked, waving the dandelion wildly with his tail, "I, Hugo, will create a *Grayling à la Redwall* such as will melt in the mouth of mice. Fresh cream! I need lots of fresh cream! Bring some mint leaves too.''

They had left Friar Hugo ranting on, delirious in his joy, as they both went off to bathe and clean up; combing whiskers, curling tails, shining noses, and the hundred and one other grooming tasks that Redwall mice always performed in preparation for an epic feast.

The rafters of Cavern Hole rang to the excited buzz and laughter of the assembled creatures: hedgehogs, moles, squirrels, woodland creatures and mice of all kinds—fieldmice, hedgemice, dormice, even a family of poor little churchmice. Kindly helpers scurried about making everybody welcome.

"Hello there, Mrs. Churchmouse! Sit the children down! I'll get them some raspberry cordial.''

"Why, Mr. Bankvole! So nice to see you! How's the back? Better now? Good. Here, try a drop of this peach and elderberry brandy.''

Matthias's young head was in a whirl. He could not remember being so happy in all his life. Winifred the otter nudged him.

"I say, Matthias. Where's this giant grayling that you and old Alf hooked, by the claw! I wish that I could land a beauty like that. Nearly a two-pounder, wasn't it?''

Matthias swelled with pride. Such praise, and from the champion fisher herself, an otter!

Tim and Tess, the twin Churchmouse babes, felt Matthias's strong arm muscles and giggled aloud in admiration. He helped to serve them two portions of apple and mint ice cream. Such nice little twins. Was it only three months ago that he had helped Sister Stephanie to get them over tail rickets? How they had grown!

Abbot Mortimer sat in his carved willow chair, beaming thanks as one by one the new arrivals laid their simple home-made gifts at his feet: an acorn cup from a squirrel, fishbone combs from the otters, mossy bark sandals made by the moles, and many more fine presents too numerous to mention. The Abbot shook his head in amazement. Even more guests were arriving!

He beckoned Friar Hugo to his side. A whispered conference was held. Matthias could only hear snatches of the conversation.

"Don't worry, Father Abbot, there will be enough for all."

"How are the cellar stocks, Hugo?"

"Enough to flood the Abbey pond, Father."

"And nuts? We must not run short of nuts."

"You name them, we've got them. Even candied chestnuts and acorn crunch. We could feed the district for a year."

"Dairy produce?"

"Oh that, I've got a cheddar cheese that four badgers couldn't roll, plus ten other varieties."

"Good, good, thank you, Hugo. Oh, we must thank Alf and young Matthias for that magnificent fish. What fine anglers they are! There's enough to keep the entire Abbey going for a week! Excellent mice, well done."

Matthias blushed to his tail's end.

"The otters! The otters!"

A loud, jolly cry went up as three otters in clown costumes came bounding in. Such acrobatics! They tumbled, balanced and gyrated, cavorting comically across the laden tabletops without upsetting as much as a single sultana. They ended up hanging from the rafters by a strand of ivy, to wild applause.

Ambrose Spike the hedgehog did his party piece. He amazed everyone with his feats of legerdemain. Eggs were taken from a squirrel's ear; a young mouse's tail stood up and danced like a snake; the incredible vanishing-shell trick was performed in front of a group of little harvest mice who kept squeaking, "He's got it hidden in his prickles."

But had he? Ambrose made a few mysterious passes and produced the shell, straight out of the mouth of an awestruck infant mouse. Was it magic?

Of course it was.

All activity ceased as the great Joseph Bell tolled out eight o'clock from the Abbey belfry. Silently, all the creatures filed to their allotted places. They stood reverently behind the seats with heads lowered. Abbot Mortimer rose and solemnly spread his paws wide, encompassing the festive board. He said the grace.

"Fur and whisker, tooth and claw,
All who enter by our door.
Nuts and herbs, leaves and fruits,
Berries, tubers, plants and roots,
Silver fish whose life we take
Only for a meal to make."

This was followed by a loud and grateful "Amen."

There was a mass clattering of chairs and scraping of forms as everyone was seated. Matthias found himself next to Tim and Tess on one paw, and Cornflower Fieldmouse on the other. Cornflower was a quiet young mouse, but undoubtedly very pretty. She had the longest eyelashes Matthias had ever seen, the brightest eyes, the softest fur, the whitest teeth. . . .

Matthias fumbled with a piece of celery and self-consciously turned to see if the twins were coping adequately. You never could tell with these baby churchmice.

Brother Alf remarked that Friar Hugo had excelled himself, as course after course was brought to the table. Tender freshwater shrimp garnished with cream and rose leaves, devilled barley pearls in acorn purée, apple and carrot chews, marinated cabbage stalks steeped in creamed white turnip with nutmeg.

A chorus of ooh's and ah's greeted the arrival of six mice pushing a big trolley. It was the grayling. Wreaths of aromatic steam drifted around Cavern Hole; the fish had been baked to perfection. Friar Hugo entered, with a slight swagger added to his ungainly waddle. He swept off his chef's cap with his tail, and announced in a somewhat pompous squeak, "Milord Abbot, honored guests from Mossflower area and members of the Abbey. Ahem, I wish to present my *pièce de résistance*—"

"Oh get on with it, Hugo!"

After some icy staring about to detect the culprit, and several smothered sniggers from around the room, the little fat friar puffed himself up once more and declaimed firmly: "*Grayling à la Redwall.*"

Polite but eager applause rippled round as Hugo sliced the fish, and placed the first steaming portion on to a platter. With suitable dignity he presented it to the Abbot, who thanked him graciously.

All eyes were on the Father Abbot. He took a dainty fork

loaded precariously with steaming fish. Carefully he transferred it from plate to mouth. Chewing delicately, he turned his eyes upwards then closed them, whiskers atwitch, jaws working steadily, munching away, his tail curled up holding a napkin which neatly wiped his mouth. The Abbot's eyes reopened. He beamed like the sun on midsummer morn.

"Quite wonderful, perfectly exquisite! Friar Hugo, you are truly my Champion Chef. Please serve our guests your master-work."

Any further speech was drowned by hearty cheers.

CHAPTER
4

Cluny was in a foul temper. He snarled viciously.

The horse had stopped from sheer exhaustion. He hadn't wanted that: some inner devil persuaded him that he had not yet reached his destination. Cluny's one eye slitted evilly.

From the depths of the hay cart the rodents of the Warlord's army watched their Master. They knew him well enough to stay clear of him in this present mood. He was violent, unpredictable.

"Skullface," Cluny snapped.

There was a rustle in the hay, a villainous head popped up.

"Aye, Chief, d'you want me?"

Cluny's powerful tail shot out and dragged the unfortunate forward. Skullface cringed as sharp dirty claws dug into his fur. Cluny nodded at the horse.

"Jump on that thing's back sharpish. Give it a good bite. That'll get the lazy brute moving again."

Skullface swallowed nervously and licked his dry lips.

"But Chief, it might bite me back."

Swish! Crack! Cluny wielded his mighty tail as if it were a bullwhip. His victim screamed aloud with pain as the scourge lashed his thin bony back.

"Mutiny, insubordination!" Cluny roared. "By the teeth of hell, I'll flay you into mangy dollrags."

Skullface scurried over on to the driver's seat, yelling with pain. "No more! Don't whip me, Chief. Look, I'm going to do it."

"Hold tight to the rigging back there," Cluny shouted to his horde.

Skullface performed a frantic leap. He landed on the horse's back. The terrified animal did not wait for the rat to bite. As soon as it felt the loathsome scratching weight descend on its exposed haunches, it gave a loud panicked whinny and bucked. Spurred on by the energy of fright it careered off like a runaway juggernaut.

Skullface had time for just one agonized scream before he fell. The iron-shod cartwheels rolled over him. He lay in a red mist of death, the life ebbing from his broken body. The last thing he saw before darkness claimed him was the sneering visage of Cluny the Scourge roaring from the jolting backboard, "Tell the devil Cluny sent you, Skullface!"

They were on the move again. Cluny was getting nearer.

CHAPTER

5

Down in Cavern Hole the great feast had slackened off.

So had a lot of belts!

Redwall mice and their guests sat back replete. There were still great quantities of food uneaten.

Abbot Mortimer whispered in Friar Hugo's ear, "Friar, I want you to pack up a large sack with food, hazelnuts, cheese, bread, cakes, anything you see fit. Give it to Mrs. Churchmouse, as secretly as you can without attracting attention. Poverty is an ugly specter when a mousewife has as many mouths to feed as she does. Oh, and be sure that her husband doesn't suspect what you are doing. John Churchmouse may be poor but he is also proud. I fear he might not accept charitable gifts."

Hugo nodded knowingly and waddled off to do his Abbot's bidding.

Cornflower and Matthias had become quite friendly. They were young mice of the same age. Though their temperaments were different they found something in common, an interest in Tim and Tess, the twin churchmice. They had passed a pleasant evening, joking and playing games with the little creatures. Tess had clambered on to Matthias's lap and fallen asleep, whereupon baby Tim did likewise in the velvety fur of Cornflower. She smiled at Matthias as she stroked Tim's small head. "Ah, bless their little paws! Don't they look peaceful?"

Matthias nodded contentedly in agreement.

Colin Vole tittered aloud and remarked rather foolishly, "Ooh, would you look at Matthias an' Cornflower there, anursin' those two babbies like they was an old wedded couple. Well, crumble my bank!''

Brother Alf reprimanded him sharply. ''Here now, you keep a latch on that silly tongue of yours, Colin Vole! Don't you know that someday Matthias will be a Redwall mouse? And don't let me hear you slandering young Cornflower. She's a decent mouse from a good family. Mark my words, Master Vole, I could say a thing or two to your mum and dad. Only last evening I saw you playing 'catch the bulrush' with that young harvest mouse. What was her name now?''

Colin Vole blushed until his nose went dry. He flounced off, swishing his tail, muttering about going outside to take the air.

Matthias caught a nod and a glance from the Abbot. Excusing himself to Cornflower, he deposited the sleeping Tess gently upon his chair and went across to him.

''Ah, Matthias, my son, here you are. Did you enjoy my Jubilee Feast?''

''Yes, thank you, Father,'' Matthias replied.

''Good, good,'' chuckled the Abbot. ''Now, I was going to ask Brother Alf or Edmund to go on a special errand, but they are no longer young mice and both look quite weary at this late hour. So, I thought I might ask my chief grayling-catcher to carry out this special task for me.''

Matthias could not help standing a bit taller.

''Say the word and I'm your mouse, sir.''

The Abbot leaned forward and spoke confidentially. ''Do you see the Churchmouse family? Well, it's such a long way back home for them on foot. Good Heavens, and there are so many of them! I thought it would be a splendid idea if you were to drive them home in the Abbey cart, along with any others going that way. Constance Badger would pull the cart, of course, while you could act as guide and bodyguard. Take a good stout staff with you, Matthias.''

The young mouse needed no second bidding. Drawing himself up to his full height, he saluted in a smart military fashion. ''Leave it to me, Father Abbot. Old Constance is a bit slow-thinking. I'll take complete responsibility.''

The Abbot shook with silent laughter as he watched Matthias march off with a soldier-like swagger. Flip flop, flip flop; he tripped and fell flat on his tail.

''Oh dear, I'll have to get that young mouse some sandals

that aren't so big," the Abbot said to himself for the second
time that day.

Well, what a stroke of luck. Fancy Cornflower's family living
so close to the Churchmouse brood! Matthias was only too glad
to offer them a lift home.

Would Miss Cornflower like to sit next to him?

She most certainly would!

Cornflower's parents sat inside the cart, her mum helping
Mrs. Churchmouse with the little ones, while her dad chatted
away with John Churchmouse as they shared a pipe of old
bracken twist.

Friar Hugo came out and dumped a bulky sack next to Mrs.
Churchmouse. "Abbot says to thank you for the loan of bowls
and tablecloths, ma'am." The fat friar gave her a huge wink.

"All comfy back there?" called Matthias. "Right, off we go,
Constance."

The big badger trundled the cart away as they called their
goodnights. She nodded at Methuselah, the ancient gatekeeper
mouse. As the cart rolled out into the road a sliver of golden
moon looked down from a star-pierced summer night. Matthias
gazed upwards, feeling as if he were slowly turning with the
silent earth. Peace was all about him: the baby mice inside the
cart whimpered fitfully in their small secret dreams; Constance
ambled slowly along, as though she were out on a nighttime
stroll pulling no weight at all; the stout ash staff lay forgotten
on the footboard.

Cornflower dozed against Matthias's shoulder. She could hear
the gentle lull of her father's voice and that of John Churchmouse, blending with the hum of nocturnal insects from the
meadow and hedges on this balmy summer night.

The Summer of the Late Rose . . . Cornflower turned the
words over in her mind, dreamily thinking of the old rambler
that bloomed in the Abbey gardens. Normally it was in full red
flower by now, but this year, for some unknown reason, it had
chosen to flower late. It was covered in dormant young rose-
buds, even now, well into June—a thing that happened only
infrequently, and usually heralded an extra-long hot summer.
Old Methuselah could only remember three other such summers
in his long lifetime. Accordingly he had advised that it be
marked on the calendar and in the Abbey chronicles as "The

Summer of the Late Rose." Cornflower's head sank lower, in sleep.

The old cart rolled on gently, down the long dusty road. They were now over halfway to the ruined Church of St. Ninian where John Churchmouse lived, as had his father, grandfather and great-grandfather before him. Matthias had fallen into a deep slumber. Even Constance was unable to stop her eyelids drooping. She went slower and slower. It was as if the little cart and its occupants were caught in the magic spell of an enchanted summer night.

Suddenly, and without warning, they were roused by the thunder of hooves.

Nobody could determine which direction the sound was coming from. It seemed to fill the very air about them as it gathered momentum; the ground began trembling with the rumbling noise.

Some sixth sense warned Constance to get off the road to a hiding place. The powerful badger gave a mighty heave. Her blunt claws churned the roadside soil as she propelled the cart through a gap in the hawthorn hedge, down to the slope of the ditch where she dug her paws in, holding the cart still and secure while John Churchmouse and Cornflower's father jumped out and wedged the wheels firmly with stones.

Matthias gasped with shock as a giant horse galloped past, its mane streaming out, eyes rolling in panic. It was towing a hay cart which bounced wildly from side to side. Matthias could see rats among the hay, but these were no ordinary rats. They were huge ragged rodents, bigger than any he had ever seen. Their heavy tattooed arms waved a variety of weapons—pikes, knives, spears and long rusty cutlasses. Standing boldly on the backboard of the hay cart was the biggest, fiercest, most evil-looking rat that ever slunk out of a nightmare! In one claw he grasped a long pole with a ferret's head spiked to it, while in the other was his thick, enormous tail, which he cracked like a whip. Laughing madly and yelling strange curses, he swayed to and fro skillfully as horse and wagon clattered off down the road into the night. As suddenly as they had come, they were gone!

Matthias walked out into the road, staff in hand. Stray wisps of hay drifted down behind him. His legs trembled uncontrollably.

Constance hauled the Abbey cart back on to the road. Cornflower was helping her mother and Mrs. Churchmouse to calm the little ones' tears of fright. Together they stood in the cart tracks amid the settling dust.

"Did you see that?"

"I saw it, but I don't believe it!"

"What in heaven was it?"

"What in hell, more like."

"All those rats! Such big ones, too."

"Aye, and that one on the back! He looked like the Devil himself."

Seeing Matthias still stunned by what had happened, Constance took over the leadership. She wheeled the cart around.

"I think we'd best head back for the Abbey," she said firmly. "Father Abbot'll want to know about this straightaway."

Knowing that the badger was far more experienced than himself, Matthias assumed the role of second-in-command. "Right, Cornflower, get in the cart and take charge of the mothers and babies," he said. "Mr. Fieldmouse, Mr. Churchmouse, up front with Constance, please."

Silently the mice did as ordered. The cart moved off with Matthias positioned on the back providing a rearguard. The young mouse gripped his staff tightly, his back to his charges, facing down the road in the direction the hay cart had taken.

CHAPTER
6

The horse had gotten away safely.

It was the hay cart that suffered most damage. Bolting reck-lessly from side to side down the road, the blinkered animal failed to see the twin stone gateposts on its right—skidding cra-zily, the cart smashed into the uprights. There was a loud splin-tering of shafts as the horse careered onwards, trailing in its wake reins, tracers and shattered timber.

His lightning reflexes serving him well, Cluny leaped clear. He landed catlike on all fours as the hay cart upended in the roadside ditch, its buckled wheels spinning awkwardly.

Feeling braced after his mad ride and the subsequent narrow escape, Cluny strode to the ditch's edge. The distressed cries of those trapped beneath the cart reached his ears. He spat con-temptuously, narrowing his one good eye.

"Come on, get up out of there, you cringing load of cats-meat," he bellowed. "Redtooth! Darkclaw! Report to me or I'll have your skulls for skittles."

Cluny's two henchrats pulled themselves from the ditch, shaking their heads dazedly.

Crack! Slash! The whiplike tail brought them swiftly to his side.

"Three-Leg and Scratch are dead, Chief."

"Dead as dirt. The cart crushed 'em, Chief."

"Stupid fools," snarled Cluny. "Serves them right! What about the rest?"

"Old Wormtail has lost a paw. Some of the others are really hurt."

Cluny sneered. "Aah, they'll get over it and suffer worse by the time I'm done with them. They're getting too fat and sluggish, by the tripes! They'd not last five minutes in a storm at sea. Come on, you dead-and-alive ragbags! Get up here and gather 'round."

Rats struggled from the ditch and the cart—frantic to obey the harsh command as quickly as possible. They crowded about the undamaged gatepost, which their leader had chosen as a perch. None dared to cry or complain about their hurts. Who could predict what mood the Warlord was in?

"Right, cock your lugs up and listen to me," Cluny snarled. "First, we've got to find out where we have docked. Let's take a bearing on this place."

Redtooth held up his claw. "The Church of St. Ninian, Chief. It says so on the notice board over yonder."

"Well, no matter," Cluny snapped. "It'll do as a berth until we find something better. Fangburn! Cheesethief!"

"Here, Chief."

"Scout the area. See if you can find a better lodging for us than this heap of rubble. Trail back to the west. I think we passed a big place on the way."

"Aye, aye, Chief."

"Frogblood! Scumnose!"

"Chief?"

"Take fifty soldiers and see if you can round up any rats that know the lie of the land. Get big strong rats, but bring along weasels, stoats and ferrets too. They'll do at a pinch. Mind now, don't stand for arguments. Smash their dens up so they won't have homes to worry about. If any refuse to join up, then kill them there and then. Understood?"

"All clear, Chief."

"Ragear! Mangefur! Take twenty rats and forage for supplies. The rest of you get inside the church. Redtooth, Darkclaw, check the armor. See if there are things about that we can use as weapons: iron spike railings—there's usually enough of them around a churchyard. Jump to it."

Cluny had arrived!

CHAPTER

7

Matthias had never stayed up all night in his life. He was just a bit tired, but strangely excited. Great events seemed to have been set in motion by his news.

Immediately upon being informed of the hay cart incident, the Abbot had insisted upon calling a special council meeting of all Redwall creatures. Once again Cavern Hole was packed to the doors, but this time it was for a purpose very different from the feast. Constance and Matthias stood in front of the Council of Elders. All about them was a hum of whispers and muttering.

Abbot Mortimer called order by ringing a small bell.

"Pay attention, everyone. Constance and Matthias, would you please tell the Council what you saw tonight on the road to St. Ninian's."

As clearly as they could, the badger and the young mouse related the incident of the rat-infested hay cart.

The Council began questioning them.

"Rats, you say, Matthias. What type of rat?" inquired Sister Clemence.

"Big ones," Matthias replied, "though I'm afraid I couldn't say what kind they were or where they had come from."

"What about you, Constance?"

"Well, I remember that my old grandad once knew a sea rat," she answered. "Going by his description, I'd say that's what they looked like to me."

"And how many would you say there were of these rats?" Father Abbot asked.

— "Couldn't say for sure, Father Abbot. There must have been hundreds."

"Matthias?"

"Oh yes, Father. I'd agree with Constance. At least four hundred."

"Did you notice anything else about them, Constance?"

"Indeed I did, Father Abbot. My badger senses told me right off that these were very bad and evil rats."

The badger's statement caused uproar and shouts of "Nonsense. Pure speculation" and "That's right! Give a rat a bad name!"

Without even thinking, Matthias raised a paw and shouted aloud, "Constance is right. I could feel it myself. There was one huge rat with a ferret's skull on a pole. I got a good look at him—it was like seeing some horrible monster."

In the silence that followed, the Abbot rose and confronted Matthias. Stooping slightly, he stared into the young mouse's bright eyes. "Think carefully, my son. Was there anything special you noticed about this rat?"

Matthias thought for a moment. Everyone was watching him.

"He was much bigger than the others, Father."

"What else? Think, Matthias."

"I remember! He only had one eye."

"Right or left?"

"Left, I think. Yes, it was the left, Father."

"Now, can you recall anything about his tail?"

"I certainly can," Matthias squeaked. "It must have been the longest tail of any rat alive. He held it in his claw as if it were a whip."

The Abbot paced up and down before turning to the assembly.

"Twice in my lifetime I have heard travelers speak of this rat. He bears a name that a fox would be afraid to whisper in the darkness of midnight. Cluny the Scourge!"

A deathly hush fell upon the creatures in Cavern Hole.

Cluny the Scourge!

Surely not? He was only some kind of folk legend, a warning used by mothers when youngsters were fractious or disobedient.

"Go to sleep or Cluny will get you!"

"Eat up your dinner or Cluny will come!"

"Come in this instant, or I'll tell Cluny!"

Most creatures didn't even know what Cluny was. He was

just some sort of bogey that lived in bad dreams and the dark corners of imagination.

The silence was broken by scornful snorts and derisive laughter. Furry elbows nudged downy ribs. Mice were beginning to smile from sheer relief. Cluny the Scourge, indeed!

Feeling slightly abashed, Matthias and Constance looked pleadingly towards the Abbot for support. Abbot Mortimer's old face was stern as he shook the bell vigorously for silence.

"Mice of Redwall, I see there are those among you who doubt the word of your Abbot."

The quiet but authoritative words caused an embarrassed shuffling from the Council Elders. Brother Joseph stood up and cleared his throat. "Ahem, er, good Father Abbot, we all respect your word and look to you for guidance, but really . . . I mean . . ."

Sister Clemence stood up smiling. She spread her paws wide. "Perhaps Cluny is coming to get us for staying up late."

A roar of laughter greeted the ironic words.

Constance's back hairs bristled. She gave an angry growl followed by a fierce bark. The mice huddled together with fright. Nobody had ever seen a snarling, angry badger at a Council meeting.

Before they could recover, Constance was up on her hind legs having her say. "I've never seen such a pack of empty-headed ninnies. You should all be ashamed of yourselves, giggling like silly little otter cubs that have caught a beetle. I never thought I'd live to see the Elders of Redwall acting in this way." Constance hunched her heavy shoulders and glared about with a ferocity that set them trembling. "Now you listen to me. Take heed of what your Father Abbot has to say. The next creature who utters one squeak will answer to me. Understand?"

The badger bowed low in a dignified manner, gesturing with her massive blunt paw. "The floor is yours, Father Abbot."

"Thank you, Constance, my good and faithful friend," the Abbot murmured. He looked about him, shaking his head gravely.

"I have little more to say on the subject, but as I see that you still need convincing, here is my proposal. We will send two mice out to relieve the gatehouse. Let me see, yes . . . Brothers Rufus and George, would you kindly go and take over from

Brother Methuselah? Please send him in here to me. Tell him
to bring the travelers' record volumes. Not the present issue, but
the old editions which were used in past years.''

Rufus and George, both solid-looking, sensible mice, took
their leave with a formal bow to the Abbot.

Through a high slitted window, Matthias could see the rosy-
pink and gold fingers of dawn stealing down to Cavern Hole as
the candles began to flicker and smoke into stubs. All in the
space of a night events had moved from festivity to a crisis, and
he, Matthias, had taken a major role in both. First the big grayling, then the sighting of the cart; large happenings for a small
mouse.

Old Brother Methuselah had kept the Abbey records for as long
as any creature could remember. It was his life's work and con-
suming passion. Besides the official chronicle of Redwall he
also kept his own personal volume, full of valuable information.
Traveling creatures, migratory birds, wandering foxes, rambling
squirrels and garrulous hares—they all stopped and chatted with
the old mouse, partaking of his hospitality, never dreaming of
hurting him in any way. Methuselah had the gift of tongues. He
could understand any creature, even a bird. He was an extraordinary old mouse, who lived with the company of his volumes
in the solitude of the gatehouse.

Seated in the Father Abbot's own chair, Methuselah took his
spectacles from a moss-bark case, carefully perching them on
the bridge of his nose. All gathered around to hear as he opened
a record book and spoke in a squeak barely above a whisper.

"Hmm, hmm, me Lord Abbot Cedric. It is Cedric, isn't it?
Oh botheration, you'll be the new Abbot, Mortimer, the one who
came after Cedric. Oh dear me, I see so many of them come
and go, you know. Hmm, hmm, me Lord Abbot Mortimer and
members of Redwall, I refer to a record of winter, six years
back.'' Here the ancient mouse took a while to leaf through the
pages. "Hmm, ah yes, here it is. 'Late in November, Year of
the Small Sweet Chestnut, from a frozen sparrowhawk come
down from the far north . . .'—peculiar chap, spoke with a
strange accent. I repaired his right wing pinfeather—' . . . news
of a mine disaster, caused by a large savage sea rat with an
extraordinary tail. It seems that this rat—Cluny they called

him—wanted to settle his army in the mine. The badgers and
other creatures who owned the mine drove them out. Cluny
returned by night, and with his band of rats gnawed away and
undermined much of the wooden shoring. This caused the mine
to collapse the next day, killing the owners.' "

Brother Methuselah closed the volume and looked over his
glasses at the assembly. "I have no need to read further, I can
recite other misdeeds from memory. As the hordes of Cluny the
Scourge have moved southwards over the past six years, I have
gathered intelligence of other incidents: a farmhouse set alight,
later that same year . . . piglets, an entire litter of them eaten
alive by rats . . . sickness and disease spread through livestock
herds by Cluny's army. There was even a report brought to me
two years ago by a town dog: an army of rats stampeded a herd
of cows through a village, causing chaos and much destruction."

Methuselah halted and blinked over his spectacles. "And you
dare doubt the word of our Abbot that Cluny the Scourge exists?
What idiotic mice you are, to be sure."

Methuselah's words caused widespread consternation. There
was much agitated nibbling of paws. Nobody could doubt he
spoke the truth; he was already old and wise when the most
elderly among them was a blind hairless mite, puling and whimpering for a feed from its mother.

"Oh my whiskers, what a mess."

"Hadn't we better pack up and move?"

"Maybe Cluny will spare us."

"Oh dear, oh dear, what shall we do?"

Matthias sprang to the middle of the floor brandishing his
staff in a way that surprised even him.

"Do?" he cried. "I'll tell you what we'll do. We'll be
ready."

The Abbot could not help shaking his head in admiration. It
seemed that young Matthias had hidden depths.

"Why, thank you, Matthias," he said. "I could not have put
it better myself. That's exactly what we will do. We'll be
ready!"

Martin the Warrior

Here is the story of Martin the Warrior, who led
his fellow beasts to victory over Badrang the
Tyrant and became Redwall's greatest hero.

CHAPTER

I

He was only a young mouse, but of strong build, with a glint in his eye that proclaimed him a born fighter. A creature of few words who never chattered needlessly. The early summer sun of the Eastern Coast beat down pitilessly on his unprotected head as he carried and stacked chunks of rock beside the masons who would shape it into blocks that would enlarge Fort Marshank.

A weasel Captain named Hisk swaggered up, cracking his long whip threateningly, looking for an excuse to cut loose on the slaves who toiled in the dusty heat around him. His eye settled on the young mouse.

"You there, liven yourself up! Come on, stir yer stumps. Lord Badrang will be round for an inspection soon. Get movin' or y'll taste my whip!"

The mouse dropped the rock he was carrying and stood staring levelly at the bullying weasel. Hisk cracked the lash viciously, the tip flicking the air a fraction from his victim's face. The young mouse did not move. His eyes hooded over as he stood in silent defiance.

The weasel Captain drew the lash back to strike, but the bold, angry eyes of the young slave seemed to challenge him. Like all bullies, the weasel was a coward at heart. Averting his gaze from the piercing stare, Hisk snapped his whip in the direction of some more timid creatures.

"C'mon, you worthless idlers, no work, no food. Move your carcasses. 'Ere comes Lord Badrang!"

Flanked by his aides, Gurrad the rat and Skalrag the fox, Badrang the Tyrant strode imperiously onto the site. He waited while two hedgehogs hurriedly built him a makeshift seat from stone blocks. Skalrag swiftly covered it with a velvet cloak. Badrang sat, gazing at the work going on around him.

The stoat Lord addressed Hisk: "Will my fortress be finished before summer is out?"

Hisk waved his coiled whip about at the slaves. "Lord, if the weather was cooler an' we 'ad more creatures . . ."

Badrang moved swiftly in his anger. Seizing a pebble, he hurled it, striking Hisk on the jaw. The weasel Captain stood dumbly, blood trickling from his lip as the Tyrant berated him.

"Excuses! I don't want to hear complaints or excuses, d'you hear me? What I need is a fortress built before autumn. Well, don't stand there snivelling, get on with it!"

Immediately, Hisk got to work, flaying about with the whip as he passed on his master's bad mood.

"Move, you useless lumps! You heard Lord Badrang, Marshank must be ready before the season's out! It'll be double the work an' half rations from now on. Move!"

An old squirrel was staggering by, bent double under the burden of a large rock. Hisk lashed out at him. The whip curled around the aged creature's footpaws, tripping him as he dropped the rock. The weasel began laying into his victim, striking indiscriminately at the old one's frail body.

"You worthless layabout, I'll strip the mis'rable hide off yer!"

The lash rose and fell as Hisk flogged away at the unprotected creature on the ground.

"I'll teach yer a lesson yer won't ferget . . ."

Suddenly the whip stopped in midswing. It went taut as Hisk pulled on the handle. He tugged at it but was yanked backwards. The young mouse had the end of the whip coiled around his paw.

Hisk's eyes bulged with temper as he shouted at the intruder, "Leggo my whip, mouse, or I'll gut yer!"

The weasel reached for the dagger at his waist, but he was not fast enough. The mouse hurled himself upon Hisk. Wrapping the whiplash round the Captain's neck, he heaved hard. Hisk thrashed furiously about in the dust, choking and slobbering as the lash tightened. Gurrad blew a hasty alarm on a bone whistle he carried slung about his neck.

In a trice the mouse was set upon by the nearest six guards. He disappeared beneath a jumble of ferrets, weasels and rats as they pounded him mercilessly, stamping upon his paws and breaking his hold on the whip. They continued relentlessly beating him with spearhandles, rods and whips until Badrang intervened.

"That's enough. Bring him to me!"

His paws pinioned by whips and a spear handle pulled hard across his throat, the young mouse was dragged struggling and kicking into the stoat Lord's presence.

Badrang drew his sword and pressed the point against the young one's heaving chest. Leaning forward, he hissed into the captive's face, "You know the penalty is death for attacking one of my horde. I could run you through with my sword right now and snuff out your life. What d'you say to that, mouse?"

The strong young mouse's eyes burned into the Tyrant's face like twin flames as he gritted out, "Scum! That sword is not yours, it belongs to me as it belonged to my father!"

Badrang withdrew the swordpoint. He sat back, shaking his head slowly in amazement at the boldness of the creature in front of him.

"Well well, you're not short of nerve, mouse. What's your name?"

The answer was loud and fearless.

"I am called Martin, son of Luke the Warrior!"

"See the roving river run
Over hill and dale
To a secret forest place,
O my heart, Noonvale.
Look for me at dawning
When the sun's reborn
In the silent beauty
Twixt the night and morn.
Wait till the lark ascends
And skies are blue.
There where the rainbow ends
I will meet you."

The mousemaid Rose sat quite still as the last tremulous notes of her song hovered on the evening air. From a vantage point in the rocks south of Marshank she looked out to sea. The water was tinted gold and scarlet from soft cloud layers, reflecting the far westering sun at her back. Below on the shore an ebbing tide gurgled and chuckled small secrets to itself as it lapped the pebbles.

"Hurr Miz Roser, you'm cumm an' get this yurr supper. Oi bain't a-cooken vittles to lay abowt an' git cold 'n' soggy. Bo urr no."

Rose's companion Grumm waved a heavy digging paw at her, and the mousemaid wandered over to join her mole friend at the low fire he had been cooking on. She sniffed appreciatively.

"Hmm, wild oatcakes and vegetable soup! Good old Grumm, you could make a banquet from nothing."

Grumm smiled, his dark velvety face crinkling around two

bright button eyes. He waved the tiny ladle which he always carried thrust through his belt like a sword.

"Hurr, an' you udd charm'ee burds outener trees with yurr sweet talken, mizzy. Set'ee daown an' eat oop."

Rose accepted the deep scallop shell full of fragrant soup. Placing her oatcake on a flat rock across the fire to keep it warm, she shook her head as she sipped away.

"You're worse than an old mousewife, Grumm Trencher. I wager you'd rock me to sleep if I let you."

Grumm wagged the small ladle at her. "Hurr aye, you'm needen all yore sleep. Urrmagine wot yore ole dad'd say iffen oi brought 'ee 'ome tired out an' a-starved, hoo arr!"

The mousemaid took a hasty bite of oatcake, fanning her mouth. "Oo, 's hot! There'll be no sleep for us until we've found out whether or not Brome is held captive in that dreadful fortress."

Grumm wiped his ladle clean with some sedge grass. "May'ap ole Brome jus' a-wandered off 'n' got losed, may'ap 'ee bain't catchered in yon fortress."

Rose shook her head.

"You must understand, Grumm, the name Brome and the word trouble go together. He was always in trouble with Father at home—that's why he went off wandering. You weren't there at the time but they had a furious argument over Brome just taking off and roaming as he pleased. Father said it was no way for the son of a Chieftain to learn his responsibilities, but Brome wouldn't listen, he ran off alone. Well, we've tracked him this far, Grumm, and I'm certain that my brother has run straight into trouble again. That's why I'm sure he's been taken by Badrang's scouts. I hope that he hasn't been forced to tell them where Noonvale is. The whole tribe of Urran Voh would be in danger if Brome gave away our location to that filthy Tyrant."

Grumm refilled Rose's shell with vegetable soup.

"Doant'ee fret, mizzy. Ole Brome can keepen his'n mouth

shutted toighter'n a mussel at low toide, ho urr!"

The mousemaid unwound the throwing sling from about her waist. "I hope you're right, Grumm. I'd hate to think of the things those vermin would do to a young mouse to get information."

The mole patted Rose's back gently with a heavy digging claw. "Doant'ee wurry, Roser. Us'll get ole Maister Brome out'n yon pest'ole iffen him be in thurr."

When they had finished eating they extinguished the fire and broke camp. A stiff breeze had sprung out of the east, bringing with it a light spatter of raindrops which threatened to get heavier as night set in.

Scrambling down the rocks, the two friends gained the shore, their paws making soft chinking noises as they trotted through the shingled tideline. Marshank stood grim and forbidding up ahead, a dark hump of misery in the moonless night.

CHAPTER

2

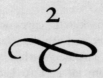

The old squirrel Martin had saved peered through the cracks of the wooden slave compound at the lone figure tied between two posts on the walltop above the main gates. His son, a burly male named Felldoh, stood behind the elder. He gritted his teeth savagely.

"The scurvy toads, they'll pay for this someday!"

Barkjon, the old one, shook his head sadly. "Martin will have a bad time tonight if the weather gets worse."

Felldoh thumped a sturdy paw against the wooden compound fence. "It's the morning I'm more worried about, when the gannets and gulls and those other big hungry sea birds come searching for food and see him tied up there. They'll rip Martin to bits!"

A weasel guard called Rotnose banged his spearbutt on the fence alongside Barkjon's nose.

"Gerraway from there, you two, or you'll be next up there with the mouse. Double work for you tomorrow. Get some sleep while you can. Sweet dreams now, hawhawhaw!"

Floodtide returned, bringing with it a storm. The gale shrieked, driving heavy rain before it. On the walltop Martin bowed his head against the battering elements. It was all that he could do, tied as he was by four paws between two thick wooden posts. Rain plastered the single frayed garment he

wore close to his body, and the wetness ran down his back,
into his ears, across his eyes and over his nose into his
mouth, battering his bowed head and numbing his whole
body, which shook and quivered in the ceaseless gale. He
hung there, like a rag doll in the wind.

Martin's mind went back to the caves on the northwest shore
where he had been born. Luke the Warrior was his father.
He had never known a mother; she had been killed in a searat
raid when he was a tiny infant. Luke had raised him the best
way he could, but Luke was a warrior and sworn to the
destruction of searats and corsairs. He was unused to rearing
babies.

Martin was only two seasons out of infancy when his father and some other warriors captured a searat galley after a
hard pitched battle on the shoreline. Flushed with success
and driven by the awful rage to take vengeance upon his
wife's murderers, Luke the Warrior gathered a crew and decided to sail off in his prize vessel, to wage war on the
searats. Martin remembered he was still very young, but fired
with a determination to accompany his father. Luke, however, would not hear of it. He left Martin in the care of his
wife's mother, Windred. The day he sailed Martin sat stone-
faced outside the cave. Luke could not reason with him.

"Son, son, you would not last two moons out there on the
high seas. I cannot risk your life pitting you in battle against
the sea scum I am sworn to do war with. Listen to me, I
know what is best for you!"

But Martin would not listen. "I want to sail on the ship
and be a warrior like you!"

Luke spread his paws wide and sighed with frustration.
"What am I going to do with you, Martin? You have my
warrior spirit and your mother's determination. Listen, son,
take my sword."

It was a fighting sword and well used. Luke pressed it into

his son's paws. The young mouse gazed wide eyed at the battle-scarred blade and gripped the handle tight as if he would never let go.

Luke smiled, recalling the time when his father had passed the sword on to him. Tapping a paw against the crosshilt, Luke said, "I can see it is in you to be a fighter, Martin. The first thing warriors must learn is discipline."

Martin felt as though the sword were speaking for him. "Tell me what to do and I will obey."

Relief surged through Luke as he commanded the would-be warrior. "You will stay and defend our cave against all comers, protect those weaker than yourself and honor our code. Always use the sword to stand for good and right, never do a thing you would be ashamed of, but never let your heart rule your mind."

He tapped the blade once more as its pitted edge glinted in the winter morning.

"And never ever let another creature take this sword from you, not as long as you live. When the time comes, pass it on to another, maybe your own son. You will know instinctively if he is a warrior. If not, hide the sword where only a true warrior who is brave of heart, would dare go to find it. Swear this to me Martin."

"I swear it, on my life!" The young mouse's grey eyes reflected the wintry sea as he spoke.

Coming back to reality, Martin lifted his head in the teeth of the gale. Was it a tear, or just rain running from his eyes as he pictured the small figure standing upon the pebbled strand alone, waving the sword in a warrior's salute as his father's ship was lost on the horizon in an afternoon of snow and icy winter spume.

Martin's head slumped onto his sodden chest as he recalled the day of his capture. Timballisto was a budding warrior, several seasons Martin's senior. He had been left in charge of the tribe by Luke. The young mouse resented his older friend's authority and often showed it by wandering far along the coast, away from the safe boundaries of the caves. It was on one such day that Martin took his father's sword, following the tideline north until the short winter afternoon began darkening. He was busy chopping away with the great blade at a driftwood log, reasoning that he could not be scolded for bringing back firewood to the cave fires.

Windred saw him from afar. She had been following his pawtracks since early noon; they stood out clearly in the smooth wet sand, marked with a straight furrow where the swordpoint trailed at Martin's side. She hurried forward scolding her grandson. "Martin! I've been out of my mind with worry. What have you been told about going off alone? D'you realize you're almost a league from the caves?"

Suddenly Windred stopped berating him. She was staring beyond Martin to where a band of villainous-looking creatures were running along the shore towards them. The old mouse threw off her shawl. "Martin, come to me. We must get away from here. Quickly!"

The young mouse turned and saw the corsairs. Dropping the firewood, he took up the sword in both paws. "Run Grandma!"

Windred would not have run anyway, but she was rooted to the spot with fear. A stoat headed the band. They stopped within two paces of their victims. The stoat grinned wickedly. "That's a big sword for a little mouse to be wielding. You'd better give it to me before you hurt yourself."

The sword was heavy and Martin's paws were tired, but he held it point forward, unwavering. "Leave us alone, stay back! My father told me never to let another creature take this sword from me!"

Now the corsairs began spreading out slowly, encircling Martin and Windred, licking knives and spearblades as they chuckled evilly at the old mouse and the small would-be warrior. The stoat took a pace forward, his voice deceptively friendly. "A wise beast your father. Did he ever tell you about those who could slay with a single spear thrust? Like this . . . or this!" As he spoke the stoat brought up his spear and began jabbing expertly at Martin. The young mouse parried, fighting off the questing spearpoint amid the laughter of the cruel corsairs.

At a nod from the stoat a weasel ran forward from behind Martin. He dealt the young mouse a heavy blow with an oaken pikestaff, laying him out flat on the sand. Badrang picked up the sword. Stepping over Martin's senseless body, he winked at Windred. She was held tight between two searats, tied and gagged by her own shawl, eyes wide with terror. The stoat stared along the swordblade at her.

"Well Grandma, he's a bold brat, that one of yours. Hmm, nice sword. It should serve me well. Hisk, we've wasted enough time. Chain these two up and get 'em back to the slavelines."

Shackled to Windred, Martin was half-dragged, half-carried further north along the wintry shore into the gathering night.

It was in the short hours before dawn that Martin came awake, shivering and moaning as a fiery drum of relentless pain beat inside his skull. Whips cracked, he was pulled upright by other slaves as the chain began moving.

Then came the long march. . . . Two seasons, trekking under the rods and whips of slavedrivers, tied by the neck to a succession of wretched creatures, all captives together. He lost count of the days. They rolled interminably on into spring, summer then autumn, with Windred long dead from hunger, thirst and hardship under the lash.

Martin recalled his grief for the old mousewife, the closest he had ever come to knowing a mother: his stifled tears and the leaden weight of sadness at her loss, the feeling of loneliness and desolation without her. She had deserved far better a fate than the one she suffered. His body began trembling at the thought of the vermin who had caused all of this cruelty.

Badrang!

The laughing, sneering, commanding stoat, swaggering along wearing the sword he had taken from Martin.

A strength born of built-up rage coursed suddenly through the young mouse. He stood erect, tugging at his bonds, oblivious to the pounding storm as a mighty roar welled up from deep inside him.

"I am a warrior! Martin son of Luke! I will live, I will not give in and die up here! Do you hear me, Badrang? I will live to take back my father's sword and slay you one day! Badraaaaaaaannggg!"

Stormwater filled his mouth, rushing winds tore at his face.

"Martin son of Luke, can you hear me?" a voice called up to him from the shore outside the fortress.

He could not see the speaker but he heard the voice clearly above the gale.

"Yes, I hear you. What is your name?"

"There are two of us, my friend Grumm Trencher the mole and myself, Laterose, daughter of the Chieftain Urran Voh. We heard you calling out. Tell me, is there a prisoner in there called Brome, a young mouse? He is my brother."

Martin could feel the storm beating the senses from him. He rallied and shouted back. "I do not know of a mouse called Brome and I don't think I'll have much chance to. I am sentenced to die up here, Laterose."

The answer came back in as kindly a tone as the mousemaid could shout under the circumstances.

"Laterose is my full title. Please call me Rose. My friend and I will do anything possible to help you, though we cannot climb up—the walls are too sheer and high. What can we do? Is there a message you wish carried to another creature?"

Martin shook his head. "No message. I am alone. The guards told me that if I live through the night the big sea birds will finish me off in the morning. Is there any way . . . you can keep them . . . off me?"

Rose thought for a moment before answering.

"Maybe, yes. We are not warriors, but we can use our slings. Also I know a trick to drive sea birds away."

She waited, but there was no reply. Grumm stepped away from the wall, out on to the beach, shading his eyes against the downpour as he gazed up at the limp figure slumped between the posts.

"Yurr, ee'm lost 'is senses, fallen aconshuss, if'n you ask oi, pore creetur!"

Rose joined Grumm, and together they watched the unconscious form sway slackly as the elements assaulted it. The mousemaid chose a hard round pebble and fitted it to her sling.

"We must help him to live, we must!" Her lip quivered as she spoke. "Ooh that Badrang, the cruel cowardly, heartless vermin . . ."

Grumm chuckled softly. "Noice wurrds fer a mouseymaid, oi must say. Hurr hurr, him'n ull live sure 'nuff, iffen 'ee be arf as ill-tempurred as 'ee, mizzy."

CHAPTER

3

Dawn came pearly grey, shot with shafts of peach and dusky pink as the sun broke the eastern horizon in the wake of the night storm. The sea was a dim shade of oily turquoise, with cream-crested waves in the middle distance. Badrang the Tyrant had his carved throne chair brought out on to the courtyard, where he could watch the fun. Gurrad the rat and Skalrag the fox stood along with two weasels called Lumpback and Stiffear, awaiting orders as the Tyrant stoat pointed to Martin's limp figure with his sword.

"He looks strong enough to have lived through a bit of wind and rain. Gurrad, go and wake the sleeping beauty. When he's conscious and wriggling about, the birds'll soon spot him."

Gurrad sniggered as he looked up at the circling sea birds that were beginning to mass above the fortress.

"Aye, Lord, that lot look in good appetite as usual, eh?"

Badrang nodded. "Never knew a gannet that wasn't. Ho there, Hisk! Don't send the slaves to the quarry yet, parade 'em out here where they can see the sentence being carried out. It'll show 'em what happens to anybeast who puts a paw wrong in my fortress."

Gurrad slapped Martin around the face with a wet piece of rag until the young mouse revived. He held a beaker of fresh water to the captive's lips, chuckling as the prisoner drank greedily.

"That's the stuff. Drink up now, mouse. Those sea birds'll soon be down for breakfast. Hehee, look at 'em, big uns, ain't they? Great pointed beaks they've got, good as a knife fer rippin' an' tearin'. They'll enjoy you . . ."

Martin managed to spit the last of the water full into Gurrad's face. The rat backed off, spluttering nastily.

"Tough, eh? Well, I 'ope they takes yer eyes first!"

Chancing a glance upwards, Martin could see a great gannet preparing to dive. Two other grey gulls were beginning to swoop low, and others rushed to join them in the descent for food. His paws were swollen by the wet ropes that held him tightly. He struggled wildly, shutting his eyes tight after Gurrad's cruel remark.

All eyes were on Martin now, the horrified slaves, the gloating horde of Badrang, the hungry sea birds. Plus two other pairs.

Rose and Grumm were crouched behind a stony outcrop on the beach, the young mousemaid watching very carefully as she placed a paw across her throat and took a deep breath. The birds wheeled and dived lower towards the struggling figure bound between the posts on the walltop. Grumm nudged his friend urgently.

"Aow, do 'asten an' 'urry, mizzy. They burds be a-goen t'peck Marthen to death. Aowurr, oi carn't lukk no moare!"

Grumm closed his eyes tight as the sea birds dived for the kill.

Badrang had forgotten to scan the seaward horizon that day, preoccupied as he was with Martin's death sentence. A sail appeared two points north on the eastern horizon. It was a great green single-masted craft, practically invisible against the sea because of its camouflaged coloring. Three banks of oars protruded to port and starboard, one atop the other, giving it the appearance of a monstrous insect crawling over the waves. It was Badrang's old partner in murder and treachery upon the high seas, a stoat like himself.

Cap'n Tramun Clogg of the great ship *Seascarab*!

Clogg was a villainous sight, an enormously fat stoat dressed in stained and tawdry silks, wearing a massive pair of carved wooden clogs. Every part of his fur wherever possible was plaited and braided—beard, eyebrows, moustache—all over his gargantuan body. Plaits and braids stuck out of his ragged sleeve frills, spilled through rents in his shirt, coat and pantaloons, even curled over the tops of the oversized clogs. He gnawed on a half-dead lobster as he slurped seaweed grog from a flagon, belching aloud and spitting shell fragments everywhere. Throwing back his tousled head he roared up at the lookout, a ferret in the crow's-nest.

"Boggs, any shape o' land out there yet, matey?"

The keen-eyed Boggs peered into the distance. "Naw, Cap'n, nary a glimmer o' . . . Wait . . . aye . . . land ahoy!"

The lobster tail fell from Tramun Clogg's open mouth, to disappear down his open shirt front.

"Haharr harr, I knowed it! Where away, Boggs y' ole bilge-dog?"

"Two points south, Cap'n. Aye, an' there be a liddle lump a-stickin' up, either a cliff or some buildin'."

Clogg gurgled happily. Drawing a broad cutlass from his sash, he began honing it on the sole of his left clog.

"Bring 'er about two points, Growch. If Badrang ain't there I'll eat me clogs, on me oath I will. Gritter, tell the crew to put some vinegar into their oarstrokes; 'urry now, matey. With this wind in our sails an' a flowin' sea, we'll make landfall soon. Hohohoharrharr! Won't me ole mess-mate Badrang be pleased ter see 'is great-uncle Clogg again after all this time!"

At the wheel Growch gave a villainous cackle. "Pleased,

yer say, Cap'n. I reckon Badrang'll pop 'is cork!"

Clogg flung the empty grog bottle over the side. "An' if he don't, I'll pop it for 'im, haharr!"

Like a great green bird of ill omen, the *Seascarab* came about and headed for Marshank as Tramun Clogg mused aloud to himself.

"Iffen I knows Badrang, 'e'll 'ave slaves aplenty, too many fer one beast to own. An ole matey like 'im won't begrudge enough fine slaves to row the *Seascarab*—'ell's teeth, I should say not. A pore lubber like me without a single slave to me vessel. Asides, tain't fittin' fer corsairs an' searats to row their own craft. So I'll just nip in nicely an' ask 'im 'andsome like to fit us out with rowbeasts. Badrang'll give 'em to me, 'e's a nice cove. An' wot if 'e don't, why then I'll just slit 'is gizzard an' take 'em, I'll use 'is skull as me figurehead an' feed the rest of 'im to the fishes. Only fair, ain't it, Growch?"

Both pirates burst out laughing at the joke. Clogg liked a joke, but he was joking in deadly earnest this time. He hated Badrang.

The sea birds came diving in voraciously at Martin's unprotected body. They were within a hair's breadth of his head when a wild, ear-splitting screech, halfway between a whistle and a cry, rent the morning air. Immediately, the scavenging birds swooped away and zoomed high into the air, shrilling anxiously and wheeling about willy-nilly. Another loud screech followed, and the gulls and gannets milled about high above Martin, some of them bumping into each other in their apparent confusion.

Badrang gaped upwards in amazement. "What's the matter with 'em, why aren't they tearing him apart?"

A further screech followed, even louder and more angry-sounding than the former two. This time the sea birds sheared off sharply and dispersed.

The Tyrant stoat was furious. "What in the name of hell-gates is going on?"

A ferret called Bluehide, who had lived in the far north, called out as he scratched his ears in puzzlement. "That's the huntin' cry of a great eagle. I've heard it afore!"

Gurrad shoved him scornfully. "Garn! There ain't no great eagles on this coast."

A small venturesome kittiwake who had just arrived on the scene took a swift dive at Martin. The screech rang out swift and harsh. The frightened kittiwake took off like a sky rocket.

Bluehide shrugged, eyeing Gurrad in a patronizing manner. "That's a great eagle's huntin' cry, I'd stake me oath on it!"

The rat raised his spearbutt threateningly. "Listen, addle-brain, I've said there ain't no gr—"

"Gurrad! Stow that gab and get over here!"

The rat broke off his argument with the ferret and scuttled across to Badrang's side. The Tyrant scowled as he glowered at the clear blue sky.

"Never mind what it is, there's something about that's scaring the sea birds witless. We'll have to tempt them down on to the mouse with a bait they can't resist. Bring a dead fish from the cookhouse."

Hurriedly the fish was brought to Badrang. He took his sword and cut the cord holding up the weasel Lumpback's ragged kilt. There was a snigger from the slaves as Lumpback stood grinning sheepishly with his only garment draped around his footpaws on the ground. Ignoring the weasel's plight, Badrang tossed the cord to Gurrad.

"Here, tie the fish to this and hang it round the mouse's neck. That'll bring hungry sea birds in to feed, eagle or no eagle."

•   •   •

From their hiding place on the shore, Rose scanned the sky. It was clear and free of sea birds.

"Thank goodness I won't have to do the eagle call again, Grumm. It was beginning to strain my throat."

"Hurr, hurr," the mole chuckled. "Oi be glad too, mizzy, 'twere a vurry froightenen sound. Oi didden loik et one liddle bit, hurr no."

Grumm peeked over the rocky outcrop at Martin on the walltop. "Mizzy Roser, 'earken! Wot be they villuns a-doin' to Marthen?"

The mousemaid began twirling her loaded sling. "I don't know, but whatever it is we'll have to stop them!"

Gurrad was trying to get the cord noose that held the fish over Martin's head, but the young mouse was ducking and struggling wildly. The rat was losing his temper.

"Hold still, mouse, or I'll pin this fish t'yer with me spear-point!"

Thwock!

Gurrad dropped the fish with an agonized yelp as the sling-stone bounced off his paw.

Badrang did not see the stone. All he saw was Gurrad dropping the fish and hopping about sucking on his paw. The Tyrant stood up, knocking his thronechair backwards as he yelled at the unfortunate rat.

"Stop playing the fool an' get that fish round his neck before I come up there and batter some sense into you with it!"

As Gurrad bent to pick the fish up, Grumm fitted a sizeable rock into the spoon of his ladle and whipped it off in the direction of the rat's bent bottom.

Thwump!

It struck hard and true, knocking Gurrad from the walltop. He plummeted over and landed with a sickening thud in the courtyard below.

Badrang leapt forward, sword in paw, waving at the creatures around him.

"To the walltop, quick. Somebeast's hurling rocks!"

They piled up the broad wooden ladders on to the walltop.

Rotnose and Hisk were first up. They were immediately hit by flying stones. Hisk fell senseless, Rotnose crouched, massaging an aching breastbone. Badrang ducked another salvo as he went into a half-stoop, shouting at the others, "Where are the stones coming from, can you see?"

Skalrag stood upright, peering at the seemingly deserted shore. "Must be somebeast hidin' out there, Lord!"

Below, at the corner of the courtyard where the slaves were grouped, the big squirrel Felldoh decided to take part in the action. He ducked to the back of the crowd, picking up several large pebbles as he went. With energy born of anger, he chucked a large rough stone at the back of Skalrag's head. Many times Felldoh had bent under Skalrag's rod; now was the chance to repay the sadistic fox.

The flying rock did not strike Skalrag's skull, it narrowly missed, but took half of his left ear in the process, ripping it off as it whizzed by. Felldoh immediately flung two more stones, then keeping his paws at his sides gazed around in amazement as if some other creature were doing the throwing.

As Skalrag screeched in pain, Stiffear sprang up, pointing down into the courtyard as he shouted excitedly, "The stones are coming from inside our own fortress!"

Thwack!

A stone from the shoreside struck him square in the back.

Rotnose, still rubbing his chest, sneered at Stiffear, "Rubbish, they're coming from the shore, I tell yer. I was hit meself. . . . Eeeyowch!"

A stone from the courtyard stung his tail. Confusion reigned on the walltop. Badrang and his creatures did not know which side the missiles were coming from. The Tyrant lay flat and raised his head slightly. He could not see the shore clearly but he had an uninterrupted view of the sea. His stomach churned suddenly and he began to curse at the sight his sharp eyes rested on. One more quick look to ascertain that he was not wrong sent Badrang scrambling for the ladder, calling hoarsely as he went, "Cut that mouse down from there and bring him with you. Get down into the fortress, quick!"

"But, Sire, we think that there's somebeast behind those rocks slinging stones . . ."

Badrang shot a venomous glance at Rotnose as he hissed, "Do as I say, scumbrain. We've more to worry about than a few stones. Tramun Clogg's out there with the *Seascarab*, sailing on a direct course for us!"

Mattimeo

Slagar the Cruel is a mysterious masked fox with a grudge against the creatures of Redwall Abbey—and a terrible plan to take his revenge.

2

Afternoon sunlight slanted through the gaps in the ruined walls and roof of Saint Ninian's old church, highlighting the desolation of weed and thistle growing around broken, rotted pews. A small cloud of midges dispersed from dizzy circling as Slagar brushed by them. The fox peered through a broken door timber at the winding path of dusty brown which meandered aimlessly southward to meet the woodland fringe on the eastern edge.

Slagar watched silently, his ragged breath sucking in and out at the purple-red diamond-patterned skull mask which covered his entire head. When he spoke, it was a hoarse, rasping sound, as if he had received a terrible throat injury at some time.

"Here they come. Get that side door open, quick!"

A long coloured cart with rainbow-hued covering was pulled into the church by a dozen or so wretched creatures chained to the wagon shaft. A stoat sat on the driver's platform. He slashed at the haulers savagely with a long thin willow withe.

"Gee up, put yer backs into it, me beauties!"

The cart was followed by a rabble of ill-assorted vermin: stoats, ferrets and weasels, garbed the same as their comrades who were already waiting with Slagar. They wore broad cloth sashes stuffed with a motley assortment of rusty daggers, spikes or knives. Some carried spears and curious-looking single-bladed axes. Slagar the Cruel hurried them along.

"Come on, shift your hides, get that door back in place quick!"

The driver jumped down from the cart.

"They're all here, Slagar," he reported, " 'cept fer that otter. He wasn't strong enough to carry on, so we finished 'im off an' chucked his carcass in the ditch, then covered it with ferns. The ants an' insects'll do the rest."

The hooded fox gave a bad-tempered snort. "So long as you weren't spotted by any creature. News travels fast in Mossflower. We've got to stay hidden now until Vitch gets back."

The twelve captives chained to the wagon shaft, mice, squirrels, voles, a couple of small hedgehogs and a young female badger, were in an emaciated condition.

One of them, a squirrel only a few seasons old, moaned piteously. "Water, please give me water."

The stoat who had been acting as driver swung his willow cane viciously at the unfortunate squirrel.

"Water? I'll give you water, you little toad. How about a taste of cane, eh? Take that!"

Slagar stepped on the end of the cane, preventing the stoat swinging it further. "Halftail, you idiot, what d'you want, slaves to sell or a load of dead flesh? Use your brain, stoat. Give the beast a drink. Here, Scringe, give 'em all a drink and some roots or leaves to eat, otherwise they'll be fit for nothing."

The ferret called Scringe leapt to do Slagar's bidding.

Halftail tugged at the willow cane to free it from Slagar's paw. The hooded fox held down harder so the stoat could not budge it.

"Now then, Halftail, me bucko, I think you're getting a bit deaf lately. I thought I told you to keep inside the woods with that cart?"

Halftail let go of the cane. "Aye, and so I did, wherever

possible," he said indignantly. "But have you tried hauling a cart and twelve slaves through that forest out there?"

Slagar the Cruel picked up the willow cane, the hood coming tight about his jaws with a sharp intake of breath. "You forget yourself, stoat. I don't have to try hauling carts, I'm the boss around here. When I looked up that path a short time ago, I saw you coming up the center of the road as if you hadn't a care in the world, bold as brass in broad daylight. Do you realize that a sentry could have seen your dust from the top of Redwall Abbey?"

Halftail failed to recognize the danger signals. "Yah, what's the difference," he shrugged. "They never saw anything."

Slagar swung the cane furiously and Halftail screamed in agony. He huddled down against the side of the cart, unable to avoid the rain of stinging cuts showering on his head, shoulders and back.

"I'll tell you the difference, slimebrain. The difference is that you don't talk back to me. I'm the leader. You'll learn that or I'll flay your hide to dollrags!" Slagar's voice grated harshly with each slash of the whipping willow.

"Whaaah mercy, ooh owow! Please stop! No more, Chief!"

Slagar snapped the cane and threw it scornfully at the stoat's heavily welted head.

"Ha, your hearing seems a little better now. Cut yourself another switch. That one's worn out."

The masked fox whirled upon his band of slavers. They sat in cowed silence. The silken hood stretched around his face as he leaned forward.

"That goes for all of you. If anyone ruins my plan, that creature will wish he'd taken his life swiftly with his own paw, by the time I'm through with him. Understand?"

There was a murmured growl of assent.

Slagar climbed up into a ruined window frame. He sat gazing in the direction of Redwall Abbey.

"Scringe, bring me some decent food and a flask of wine from the cart," he commanded.

The servile ferret ran to obey his master.

"Threeclaws, station yourself outside at twilight. Keep
an eye peeled for Vitch coming back."

The weasel saluted. "Righto, Chief."

The afternoon wore on, peaceful and golden. Now and then
a small dust devil swirled on the path with the summer heat.

Slagar ran a paw tenderly over the silk harlequin-
patterned hood, smiling beneath it as a plan of revenge
against Redwall revolved slowly in his twisted mind.

Vengeance had kept him going for a long time now.
Sometimes he actually savoured the burning lances of pain
that coursed through his face, knowing the day was approaching when he would pay back those he considered
responsible for his injuries.

A beetle trundled out of the pitted, rotten woodwork of
the window frame. Slagar the Cruel pierced it neatly with
a single claw, watching the insect writhe in its death throes.
"Redwall, heeheeheehee!" The fox's laughter sent shud-
ders through every creature present.

3

"Mattimeo, Mattimeo!"

Cornflower wrung her paws distractedly. She took one last look around Cavern Hole before climbing the stairs to Great Hall. It was quiet and cool in the Abbey's largest room. Shafts of sunlight, multi-coloured from the stained-glass windows, lanced downwards, etching small pools of rainbow-hued light on the ancient stone floor.

The mouse wandered outside, murmuring beneath her breath as she bustled along, "Where has the little snip gone this time, I wonder? Oh, Matti, you'll have me grey before my time."

John Churchmouse was climbing rather stiffly down from the west wall stairs with his book and quill. He almost bumped into Cornflower as she crossed the grounds.

"Afternoon, ma'am. My, my, you look busy."

Cornflower sat upon the bottom step and heaved a huge sigh. She fanned her whiskers with her paw. "Busy isn't the word for it, Mr. Churchmouse. I've spent the last hour looking for that son of mine. You haven't seen him, by any chance?"

The kindly recorder patted Cornflower's paw. "There, there, don't you worry your head, ma'am. If your little

Matti is anywhere, he'll be with my Tim and Tess. Young
rips, they were supposed to be helping Brother Rufus to
write out place names for the table. Ha, there he is now.
Hi, Rufus, seen anything of Tim, Tess or young Matti
lately?''

Brother Rufus strode across, shaking his head. He wag-
gled a scroll of birchbark parchment at them both.

''Ruined!'' he exclaimed. ''Just look at this list they're
supposed to have written. I can't possibly use any of this
for place settings. Look, Abbot Mordalfus, spelt with one
'b.' Basil Stag Hare, you'd think that was simple enough.
Oh no, they've spelt Basil 'Bazzerl' and put an 'e' on the
end of Stag!''

John Churchmouse pulled forth a kerchief. He blew his
snout loudly to disguise the laughter that was shaking him.
''Hmm, yes, ahaha. 'Scuse me, well, that wouldn't have
been my Tess, you know. She's quite good at the spelling.''

Brother Rufus rolled the parchment tightly. ''It's that little Mattimeo, he's the ringleader. I know you may not like
that, Cornflower marm, but it's the truth!'' His voice was
shrill with frustration.

Cornflower nodded her head sadly. ''Yes, I'm afraid I
must agree with you, Brother Rufus. Matti is becoming a
real problem. I daren't tell his father half the things he gets
up to.''

John Churchmouse peered sympathetically over the top
of his square eyeglasses. ''Maybe it'd be better to do so, if
you'll excuse me for saying. Young Matti will have to start
growing up sometime if he ever hopes to become the Warrior of Redwall like his father Matthias. Mattimeo will have
to start behaving responsibly instead of going about like a
spoilt brat, if you'll pardon the expression, ma'am.''

Cornflower stood up. ''I know exactly what you mean,
Mr. Churchmouse, but we may be judging Matti a little
unfairly. After all, he does have quite a lot to live up to,
being the son of Redwall's Warrior. Besides, practically
every woodlander within our walls has spoiled him since
the day he was born.''

Both John and Rufus nodded their heads in agreement.

The awkward silence which followed was immediately broken by a band of small creatures headed by a young mole who waved his digging claws wildly.

"Cumm yurr quickly, gennelmice, 'asten ee. Li'l Matti be a-slayin' Vitch. Do 'urry!"

Even though the little creature was speaking in the quaint and complicated molespeech, they understood the urgency of his message.

"Where, where?" they cried. "Take us there quickly!"

The group dashed around the south Abbey gable, taking the shortcut to the east grounds.

Cornflower picked up her skirts, narrowly avoiding collision with a baby hedgehog. Brother Rufus was out in front.

Jess Squirrel was first on the scene. She had been up an apple tree in the orchard with her son Sam when they heard the screams. Travelling from bough to bough, swift as a bird in flight, Jess dropped to the ground and set about trying to separate the two creatures locked together on the grass. They rolled, kicked, spat and bit furiously. Sam dropped down to his mother's aid. They grabbed one each and held them apart. As they did, the crowd arrived.

Mattimeo was panting heavily. He tried to break free, but Jess shook him soundly by the scruff.

"Be still, you little ruffian, or I'll tan your hide!" she warned him.

Sam held tight to the other mouse, Vitch, who looked more like a rat, small though he was. Vitch was not struggling. He looked quite relieved that the fight had been stopped.

John Churchmouse strode firmly between them. "Now then, what's all this about, eh?"

"He called me a skinny little rat."

"He said I was not a warrior's son."

"He pulled my tail and he jumped on me and bit me and—"

"Silence!"

Every creature present froze at the booming growl of a huge grey female badger. Constance, the mother of all Redwall, stood high on her hind legs, towering above them. Folding her front paws judiciously, she glared down at the two small miscreants.

"Vitch, is it? Well, Vitch, you are a newcomer to our Abbey, but that is no excuse for fighting. We are peaceable creatures at Redwall. Violence is never the answer to a quarrel. What have you got to say for yourself?"

The ratlike mouse wiped a smear of blood from his snout.

"It was Mattimeo," he whined piteously. "He hit me first, I wasn't doing anything, I was just . . ."

Vitch's faltering excuses faded to a whimper under the badger's stern gaze. She pointed a blunt paw at him.

"Go to the kitchens. Tell Friar Hugo that I sent you. He will set you to sweeping floors and scrubbing pans. I will not have fighting in the Abbey, nor whimpering, whining and trying to put the blame upon others. Brother Rufus, take him along, see he delivers my message to Friar Hugo properly."

Vitch looked as if he were about to dodge off, until Brother Rufus caught him firmly by the ear and marched him away.

"Come on, young Vitch, greasy pots and floor scrubbing will do you the world of good."

"Owowooch, leggo, you big bully," Vitch protested. "You're pulling my ear off!"

When Vitch had gone, Constance turned upon the other culprit. Jess had released Mattimeo. He stood shamefaced, kicking at a clump of turf, looking down at his paws. He did not see the nod which passed between his mother and Constance. Cornflower was giving her silent permission to the badger; Mattimeo was in for a dressing-down.

"Son of Matthias the Warrior, look at me!" Constance commanded.

Sheepishly the young mouse gazed upward until he was staring into Constance's unblinking dark eyes. The onlookers stood silent as the matriarch gave the young mouse a piece of her mind.

"Mattimeo, this is not the first time I have had cause to speak with you. I am not going to ask you for an explanation, because in this case I do not think you could justify yourself. Vitch is a newcomer, hardly arrived here. You were born at Redwall, you know the rules of our Abbey: to live in peace with others, never to harm another creature needlessly, to comfort, assist, and be kind to all."

Mattimeo's lip quivered, he looked as if he were about to speak, but the badger's stern gaze silenced him.

"Today you took it upon yourself to attack another creature who is a guest in our home," Constance continued, her voice an accusing knell. "You, the son of my old friend Matthias the Warrior, who fought to bring peace to Mossflower. Mattimeo, I will not give you any tasks to do as a punishment. The sorrow and worry you cause your mother and the shame you bring down upon your father are the penalties that will rest on your own head. Go now and speak with your father."

Mattimeo's head drooped low as he stumbled off.

Tess, Tim and Sam Squirrel kept silent. They knew that every word Constance spoke was the truth. Mattimeo's middle name should have been trouble.

4

The new moon was up. It hung like a fresh-minted coin in a still, cloudless sky of midnight blue. Moths fluttered vainly upward, only to drift spiralling down to the grass-carpeted woodland floor. The trees stood like timeless sentinels. Somewhere a nightjar serenaded the soft darkness.

Threeclaws was alert at his sentry post. He spied the figure of Vitch approaching and gave a low whistle.

The undersized rat looked up. "Where's Slagar and the others?" he asked.

Threeclaws pointed with his dagger. "Inside the church. What've you been doing to yourself?"

"Keep your snout out of my business, fatty," said Vitch, dodging nimbly past Threeclaws into the church.

Weasels and a few ferrets and stoats lay about sleeping on the floor. Slagar sat with his back against the painted cart. He scowled at Vitch.

"You took your time getting here. What in the name of the fang kept you?"

Vitch flung himself wearily on a tattered hassock. "Washing dirty pots and greasy pans, scrubbing floors and generally getting meself knocked about."

Slagar crouched forward. "Never mind all that. I put you

in there to do a job. When is the feast to begin?''

"Oh that. One more moonrise, then the early evening following.''

"Right, did you fix the bolts on the small north wall-gate?'' asked Slagar.

"Of course. That was the first thing I attended to. They're well greased and fit for a quick getaway. You can keep that Redwall place, Slagar. I'm not goin' back there again.''

"Oh, why's that, Vitch?'' The fox's voice was dangerously gentle.

"Huh, it was hard enough tryin' to pass meself off as a mouse. That young one, wotsisname? Matty something—he smelt a rat right away. I had a fight with the little nuisance. He's strong as an otter. Then I was pulled up by a big badger. She gave me a right old tellin' off. Peaceful creatures, my front teeth! I was lugged off and made to scrub dirty pots for some fat old cook. He had me up to my tail in greasy dishwater, standin' over me and makin' me scour and cl—''

"Ah shut your trap and stop snivelling, rat. This little mouse, was he called Mattimeo, son of Matthias the Warrior?''

"Aye, that's him, but how do you know?''

Slagar touched the red silk skull cover, baring his fangs viciously. "Never mind how I know. He's the one we'll be taking away with us, him and any others we can lay our paws on.''

Vitch brightened up. "Maybe I'll get a few minutes alone with Mattimeo after we make our getaway, when he's chained up good and proper.''

Slagar watched the small rat's face approvingly. "Ha, you'd like that, wouldn't you?''

"Heehee, like it, I'd love it!'' Vitch's eyes shone malevolently.

The fox leaned closer. "Vengeance, that's the word. I tell you, rat, there's nothing in the world like the moment when you have your enemy helpless and you can take revenge.''

Vitch was puzzled. "I can't imagine a little mouse like that being able to hurt you, Sly One. What did he do that you seek revenge upon him?"

Slagar had a faraway look in his eyes, and beneath the mask his breath hissed roughly.

"It was his father, the Warrior, that big badger too—in fact, it was all the creatures at Redwall who hurt me. The little one was not even born then, but I know how they all dote on him. He is the son of their warrior, the hope of the future. I can kill a lot of birds with one stone by taking Mattimeo. You couldn't imagine the agonies they'd go through if he went missing. You see, I know the woodlanders of that Abbey. They love their young and they'd rather be made captive themselves than have anything happen to their precious little ones. This is what will make my revenge all the sweeter."

Suddenly Vitch stretched a paw towards Slagar's masked face. "Did they do that to you? Is that why you have to wear a mask over your head? Why don't you take it o— Aaaarrrggghh!"

Slagar seized Vitch's paw and bent it savagely backwards. "Don't you ever dare put your grubby paw near my face again, or I'll snap it clean off and make you eat it, rat! Now get back to that Abbey and keep your eyes open. Make sure you know exactly where that young mouse is at all times, so that I can put my paw on him when the moment arrives."

He released Vitch and the small rat huddled on the ground, sobbing. Slagar spat on him contemptuously. "Get up, misery guts. If you're still lying there in a moment, you'll feel my sword. That really will give you something to moan about."

Vitch picked himself up slowly and painfully. Next moment he was sent hurtling by a kick on the behind from Slagar.

"Garn! Get yourself out of my sight, you snivelling snot-face."

Vitch departed hastily, leaving Slagar to take his ease once more. The Cruel One lay back, all thoughts of sleep banished by one word which echoed around his twisted mind like an eerie melody.

Revenge!

Matthias the Warrior of Redwall stood with his back to the empty fireplace. Cornflower had gone out early to help with the baking. Golden morning sunlight streamed through the windows of the small gatehouse cottage, glinting off the dewy fruit piled upon the table. There was a pitcher of cold cider, some cheeses and a fresh-baked loaf set out for breakfast but Matthias lacked the appetite to do it justice and stared miserably about the room. It was neat and cheerful, which did not reflect the Warrior's mood.

There was a knock on the door.

"Come in, please," he called, straightening up.

The Foremole entered, tipping the top of his black velvet furred head with a huge digging claw. He wrinkled his button nose in a wide smile that almost made his bright little eyes vanish.

"Gudd morn to you'm, Mattwise, yurr. Uz moles be diggen a cooker pit t'day. May'aps you'ud loik to 'elp?"

Matthias smiled fondly. He patted his old friend's back, knowing the mole had come to cheer him up.

"Thank you for the offer, Foremole. Unfortunately I have other more serious business to attend this morning.

Hmm, that sounds like it in the next room, just getting out of bed. Will you excuse me, my friend?''

"Hurr hurr, ee be a roight laddo, yurr young Mattee. Doant wack 'im too 'ard naow," Foremole chuckled, and left to join his crew.

Matthias had been far too angry to deal with his son on the previous afternoon, so he sent him straight off to bed without tea or supper. Now the Warrior stood facing the bedroom door, watching the tousled head of his son peer furtively around the door jamb.

Seeing his father, he hesitated.

"Come in, son." The Warrior curled a paw at him.

The young mouse entered, gazing hungrily at the laden breakfast table before turning to face his father. Sternness had replaced the previous day's anger on the Warrior's face.

"Well, what have you got to say for yourself, Mattimeo?"

" 'm sorry," Mattimeo mumbled.

"I should hope you are."

" 'm very sorry," Mattimeo mumbled again.

"Foremole said I should whack you. What do you think?"

" 'm very very sorry. 't won't happen again, Dad."

Matthias shook his head, and placed a paw on his son's shoulder.

"Matti, why do you do these things? You hurt your mother, you hurt me, you hurt all our friends. You even get your own little pals into trouble. Why?"

Mattimeo stood tongue-tied. What did they all want? He had apologized, said he was very sorry, in fact, he would never do it again. Jess Squirrel, his mother, Constance, they had all given him a stern telling-off. Now it was his father's turn. Mattimeo knew that the moment he set paw out of doors he would be spotted, probably by Abbot Mordalfus, and that would mean another stern lecture.

Matthias watched his son carefully. Beneath the sorrow-

ful face and drooping whiskers he could sense a smoulder-
ing rebellion, resentment against his elders.

Turning to the wall over the fireplace, Matthias lifted
down the great sword from its hangers. This was the sym-
bol of his rank, Warrior of Redwall. It was also the only
thing that could command his son's total attention. Matthias
held the weapon out.

"Here, Matti, see if you can wield it yet."

The young mouse took the great sword in both paws.
Eyes shining, he gazed at the hard black bound handle with
its red pommel stone, the stout crosstree hilt and the magnificent blade. It shone like snowfire, edges sharp and keen
as a midwinter blizzard, the tip pointed like a thistle spike.

Once, twice, he tried to swing it above his head. Both
times he faltered, failing because of the sword's weight.

"Nearly, Father, I can nearly swing it."

Matthias took the weapon from his son. With one paw
he hefted it, then swung it aloft. Twirling it, whirling it
until the air sang with the thrum of the deadly, wonderful
blade. Up, down and around it swung, coming within a
hair's-breadth of Mattimeo's head. Turning, Matthias
snicked a stalk from an apple, sliced the loaf without touching the table and almost carelessly flicked the rind from the
cheese. Finally Matthias gave the sword a powerful twist
into the warrior's salute, bringing the blade to rest with its
point quivering in the floor.

Admiration for the Warrior of Redwall danced in his
son's eyes. Matthias could not help smiling briefly.

"One day you will be the one who takes my place, son.
You will grow big and strong enough to wield the sword,
and I will train you to use it like a real warrior. But it is
only a sword, Mattimeo. It does not make you a warrior
merely because you carry it. Weapons may be carried by
creatures who are evil, dishonest, violent or lazy. The true
Warrior is good, gentle and honest. His bravery comes from
within himself; he learns to conquer his own fears and misdeeds. Do you understand me?"

Mattimeo nodded. Matthias grew stern once more.

"Good, I am glad you do. I will not whack you. I have

never laid a paw on you yet and I do not intend starting now. However, you attacked little Vitch and you must pay for that, one way or another. At first I thought I should refuse you permission to attend the celebrations. . . .''

Matthias watched the shock and disbelief on his son's face before continuing.

''But I have decided that you may go, providing you run straightaway to the kitchens. There you will ask Friar Hugo to allot you double the tasks he gave to Vitch yesterday. When you have finished working for the Friar, you will offer to help your mother with the gathering of flowers until such time as she decides to free you of your task. Is that clear?''

Mattimeo's face was a picture of disbelief. He, the son of the Redwall Warrior, working! Never before had he been asked, much less ordered, to carry out Abbey tasks. The young mouse considered himself the inheritor of his father's sword and duties. As such, he was firmly convinced that he was above any type of pan-scrubbing or daisy-gathering. Even Constance knew that. She had sentenced Vitch to hard labour, but even she did not dare tell the future Champion to dirty his paws with menial chores. Besides, Vitch would be finished with his tasks by now. He could stand about and gloat at the sight of his enemy ordered to perform double the work and more.

Matthias watched his son's face. Now was the testing time. Would he behave like the spoiled little creature who had been indulged all his life by the Abbey dwellers, or would he show a bit of character?

The young mouse swallowed hard, nodding his head. ''I'll do as you have asked, Dad.''

Matthias clapped him heartily on the back. ''Good mouse. That's the mark of a warrior in training, obedience. Off you go now!''

Morning sunlight stencilled the high window shaped in soft pink relief on the sandstone floor of Great Hall as Mattimeo passed through on his way to the kitchens. He felt the fur on his shoulders prickle slightly, as if some beast were watching him from behind. Turning slowly, he faced the west wall. No creature was there. The hall was empty, save for the picture of Martin the Warrior upon the Redwall tapestry. Mattimeo often had this same experience when he was alone and near the large woven cloth. He drew closer, standing in front of the magnificent armoured mouse's likeness. Martin the Warrior looked big and strong. He held the famous sword easily in his right paw, a smile upon his broad honest face, and behind him the images of bygone enemies fled in fear as if trying to escape from the tapestry. The young mouse's eyes glowed in admiration of his hero. He spoke to Martin, not knowing that his father Matthias had done the same thing when he was young.

"I could feel you watching me, Martin. I'm just on my way to do penance in the kitchens, but you probably know that. I didn't mean to disobey my parents or cause them unhappiness. You can understand that, can't you? I had to fight Vitch because he said things about my father. He thought I was scared of him, but I am the son of a warrior and I could not let him insult my family. If my father knew the truth of it all he would not have punished me, but, well, he's my father, you see. I can't explain things properly to him. You're different, Martin. You understand how I feel."

Mattimeo shuffled his paws on the stones beneath Martin's never changing expression.

"You know, sometimes you're just like my father. Look, I'm sorry, I'll try to be a better mouse. I promise not to fight or get into any more trouble or worry my parents again."

He turned and shuffled sulkily toward the kitchens, muttering as he went, "I wish there was another Great War, then I'd show 'em. Huh! They'd be glad of young mice that could fight then. I wouldn't be sent off to scour pans. They'd probably have to give me a medal or something like that."

The smile upon the face of the tapestry warrior seemed to be gentler as the immobile eyes watched the small habit-clad figure descend the steps of Cavern Hole.

Mariel of Redwall

Mariel and her father are captured and thrown overboard by Gabool the Wild, vicous pirate king of the searats. But they survive to find a home at Redwall Abbey, and to make Gabool pay for his crimes!

1

Abbot Bernard folded his paws deep into the wide sleeves of his garb.

From a viewpoint on the threshold of Redwall Abbey's west ramparts he watched the hot midsummer day drawing to a glorious close. Late evening light mellowed the red sandstone Abbey walls, turning them to dusty scarlet; across the flatlands, cloud layers striped the horizon in long billows of purple, amber, rose and cerise. Bernard turned to his friend Simeon, the blind herbalist.

"The sun is sinking, like the tip of a sugar plum dipping into honey. A perfect summer evening, eh, Simeon?"

The two mice stood silent awhile before Simeon turned his sightless face toward the Abbot.

"Father Abbot, how is it that you see so much yet feel so little? Do you not know there is a mighty storm coming tonight?"

The Abbot shook his head, disbelieving, yet unwilling to deny Simeon's unerring instinct. "A storm? Surely not!"

Simeon chided Abbot Bernard gently. "Perhaps you

have other things on your mind, my friend. Maybe you have not felt the cooling breezes die away. The air has become still and hot, the birds stopped their evensong much earlier than usual, even the grasshoppers and the buzzing bees have ceased what little noise they make. Listen!"

The Abbot cocked his head on one side, perplexed. "I hear nothing."

Simeon chuckled dryly. "That is because you are hearing the sound of silence, Bernard. One thing I have learned in my life is to listen to the sounds of Mossflower country. Every sound carries information; so does every silence. This is going to be a mighty storm, one that we have not seen the like of in many a long season."

Taking Simeon by the paw, Abbot Bernard led his blind companion down the rampart steps and across the lawn toward the main Abbey building.

Simeon sniffed the air. "Mmmm! I smell hot apple pie and raspberry cream pudding, and scones, fresh from the oven too, with damson preserve spread on them. We'd best hurry before the moles get here or there'll be none left."

The Abbot quickened his pace. "How d'you know the moles are coming?"

"Bernard, Bernard, did you ever know Sister Sage to serve raspberry cream pudding and no moles to arrive?"

"Right again, Simeon. Your powers of observation leave me in the shade. Oh, I must tell young Dandin to beat the log alarm. It'll warn anybeast still outdoors to come in."

Simeon grimaced. "Oh dear, do we have to suffer that noise again? Young Dandin is a bit overenthusiastic at beating a hollow log with two clubs."

Abbot Bernard smiled reflectively. "Yes, he does rather put his heart into it, doesn't he. Still, I wish everyone were as willing in their duties as our Dandin. If ever Redwall Abbey gets a bell, I'll be the first to vote him as bellringer."

The two mice made their way between the flowerbeds

which dotted the dark greensward. An ominous grumble
of thunder muffled its way over the far horizon to the
northwest. Abbot Bernard turned in the doorway of the
Abbey, attempting to conjure up his powers of smell.

"Hmmm, cider poured cold from the cask, eh, Simeon?"

The blind herbalist wrinkled his nose. "Wrong, it's
pear cordial."

The Father Abbot of all Redwall tried not to look
amazed. Even though Simeon could not see him, he
might sense his Abbot's expression.

Far, far over the horizon, far to the northwest, far across
the oily blue green billows which were rising, lashing
their tops into rippling white peaks of foam, far over the
abysses and deeps of the heaving seas, far from the peace
and calm of Redwall Abbey, stood Gabool the Wild.

Clouds of jet black and slate gray boiled down out of
the sky to meet the lashing waves. A blast of hot wind
like the gust from hell-furnace doors set Gabool's scarlet
cape fluttering as he stood on the high cliffs of his island,
defying the elements. Thunder boomed out, forked lightning ripped through the lowering vault of the sky. Gabool
drew his jewel-hilted sword and waved it at the storm as
he roared and laughed in exultation. The deadly curved
blade with its sharp double edges hummed and sang
against the wind.

Gabool the Wild ruled the seas, he was the dread Lord
of Terramort Island, King of the Searats, Warlord of all
Rodent Corsairs, Captain of Captains. No creature alive
was a fiercer fighter than Gabool. From the lowly posi-
tion of a young scullyrat he had fought his way up to be
the biggest, the most savage, the cruelest and the most
ruthless. In all the seas and oceans there had never been
a rat like Gabool the Wild. Huge gold hoops dangled
from his ears, his fangs (which he had lost long ago in
hard-fought combat) were replaced by sharp jutting gold
canines, each one set with a glinting green emerald. Below his weird yellow blood-flecked eyes, an enormous

dark beard sprouted and curled, spilling down to his broad chest, silk ribbons of blue and red woven through it. Whenever Gabool moved, his rings, bracelets, medals and buckles jangled. Gold, turquoise, silver, ivory—plunder from the far places of the high seas. Strange weapons with shimmering twisted blades were thrust into the purple sash about his waist. Dangerous to serve and deadly to trust, he stood laughing in the teeth of the gale, satisfied that the creature who had dared go against him was now fish bait on the seabed. Thunder crashed overhead as the skies released a deluge of whipping, lashing rain. Lightning crackled around the rocky tor, illuminating the barbaric figure as if even the high heavens were challenging him.

The Warlord of all Waters threw back his huge head and shrieked out his battle cry to the storm.

"Gaaaaboooool!"

The pitifully tiny figure of a mousemaid was hurled about like a chip of bark in the eastward rush of high roaring seas. Tormented rolling waves, whipped to a frenzy by the screeching wind, billowed and swelled, long combing chariots pulled fiercely along by tossing white stallions of foam and spray.

The mousemaid, partially stunned, dared not even let one paw free to undo the rope about her neck. Her numbed paws clung grimly to a jagged spar of driftwood as she plunged wildly about in the maddened waters, now on top of a wave high as a castle, hurtling down blue green valleys into a trough that yawned like a deep, dark monster mouth, now being spun sideways with the spume, now being flung backwards from greater heights to vaster depths.

The rope became tangled around the wooden spar; painfully the little maid tried to bite at the hemp. Seawater gushed into her mouth, and she retched as the water threatened to choke her. A flailing end of rope struck her across the eyes. Unthinkingly she let go of the spar; it whipped off in a different direction from her. With both

paws tearing feebly at the rope circling her neck, she was
shaken about like a small fish upon rod and line.

All consciousness was finally beaten from her body
when the spar struck her across the head, and the helpless
figure was lost amid the pounding crashing seas. Ob-
scured by the boiling cloud curtains above the maelstrom,
not even the stars or moon were witness to the fate of
the little mousemaid, victim of Gabool's cruel whim. . . .

Fort Bladegrit stood at the edge of the high rocks which towered above Terramort cove, the big window of its banqueting hall facing out to sea. It had a courtyard and a high wall which ran around its perimeter where the ground was open, though part of the actual fort building integrated with the outer wall where it overhung the cove. The entire structure was built from solid rock with heavy wooden doors at the entrances both to the fort and courtyard. On three sides it was overlooked by hills. Gabool the Wild had taken it as his by right; indeed whoever owned Bladegirt was absolute King of Searats, as long as he could hold it. Inside the fort chaos and misrule were the order of the day. Corsair rats left their ships to come ashore after long plundering voyages. They made their way to Bladegirt in droves, leaving their ships at anchor in the cove. Roistering, fighting, gambling and drinking, the searats enjoyed their shore leave after the hardships of a life at sea.

In the high banqueting chamber Gabool sprawled on a carved rock throne, which he had made more comfortable by covering it with the skins of his slain enemies. He

stared with loving fascination at a great bell dominating
the center of the floor; monumental in its size the prize
stood, reflecting the torchlights and revelry through its
burnished sheen. Copper, silver, brass and gold had been
used in its casting. Heaving himself up, Gabool strode
forward, sword in one claw, a chalice of wine in the other
as he traversed the perimeter of his greatest prize. Grinning like a child with a new toy, he tapped his sword-
blade against the marvelous bell; the soft musical note
vibrated gently like a giant harp strummed by the wind.
As he walked, Gabool's restless eyes roved up and down,
from the strange figures embossed around the top to the
intricate words ranging around the wide base of the great
bell.

Gabool was puzzled as to their meaning, but they were
pretty decorations which made his prize all the more fas-
cinating to look upon.

"Blood 'n' thunder, Cap'n. Give it a good belt an' let's
hear it ring out!" A burly drunken searat named Halfnose
pulled a wooden cudgel from his belt and thrust it toward
Gabool. With lightning speed the Warlord grabbed the
club and crashed it down on Half-nose's skull, at the
same time landing a thrusting kick into the drunkard's
belly, which sent him reeling into an open cask of wine.
Halfnose slumped across the wine, his head submerged.
Gabool roared with laughter.

"Drink or drown, seascum. Nobeast comes near Gabool's bell!"

The carousing searats shrieked their appreciation at his
joke. Gabool pointed at Halfnose with his sword.

"If he ever gets out o' there, give him a cup of wine
t' revive him."

This caused further merriment, except from the table
where Bludrigg, Captain of the ship *Greenfang*, sat with
his mates. Though Gabool laughed as heartily as the others, Bludrigg had not escaped his notice. Everyone was
laughing, but not Bludrigg—Bludrigg the surly, Bludrigg
the argumentative, Bludrigg the trouble-causer, the sea-
deck lawyer. Gabool watched him closely. Bludrigg, who

could sense the scheming mind behind his King's false merriment.

Things between the King of Searats and his Captain had been building to a head for a long time; Gabool decided to settle accounts with Bludrigg now. Gulping wine from the chalice and allowing it to spill freely into his beard, Gabool pretended to stagger drunkenly. He winked in a friendly manner and thrust his sword point down into a chest of booty. Tottering over to the table, Gabool banged the half-empty chalice down in front of the *Greenfang*'s Captain.

"Bludrigg, me old matey, c'mon, drink up!"

Bludrigg's face was sullen as he thrust the chalice aside.

"Don't want no wine. I can drink all I want aboard me ship."

All around the hall they stopped drinking, singing and gambling; an air of expectancy settled over the searats. Gabool blinked, as if trying to shake off the effects of the wine, and swayed slightly.

"Food then. Can't have my Captain starvin'. Roast meat, fruit, fish, sugared preserves? Here, bring m' friend Bludrigg some vittles."

Bludrigg's swordclaw fondled the hilt of his sheathed scimitar.

"Leave the food, Gabool. I eat well enough."

Gabool sighed, shaking his head as if in puzzlement. He sat next to Bludrigg and threw a comradely claw about his shoulders.

"Hmmm, no wine, no food, no smile on me old shipmate's face. What d'you want then, bucko?"

Bludrigg shook Gabool's claw off. He stood upright, knocking the chair over behind him, his eyes blazing with suppressed rage at the drunken Warlord.

"I want my share of the plunder. There's been none from the last three sailings. I'm tellin' you, Gabool, I want my portion of the booty—an' I'll have it tonight, come hell or high water!"

From around the packed hall there were murmurs of

agreement. Gabool spread his arms wide and smiled.

"Blow me down! Is that all? Why didn't you say so sooner?"

Bludrigg was lost for words; the expected clash had not come. Now he felt slightly foolish in front of his crew. He shrugged, mumbling halfheartedly; he tried excusing himself as if he were complaining on behalf of his searats.

"Well, I never thought. . . . It's just that my crew were startin' to complain, they thought you'd forgotten us . . ."

Gabool looked injured. He went over to the chest of booty, where his sword stood upright amid a heap of armlets, goblets, baubles and shiny stones. Drawing forth the sword, he turned one or two items over with its point until he found what he sought. Gabool flicked the sword up as a shiny gold coronet studded with gems slid along its blade.

"Aharr, friend Bludrigg, the best for you. A crown fit for a King!"

Bludrigg felt a sudden rush of confidence; he had done it! Gabool was notoriously mean with plunder, but he, Bludrigg, Captain of the *Greenfang*, had actually got the better of Gabool. The King of Searats had backed down before him. Bludrigg's chest swelled as he accepted the beautiful coronet from Gabool's sword-blade and placed it on his head. A cheer rose from the company as Gabool spread his arms wide. Extending the sword away from Bludrigg, he addressed them.

"See, yer scurvy wave-riders. Pay attention, you jetsam of the oceans, I am Gabool the Wild, this is how I repay me friends. . . ." Without warning Gabool swung a powerfully savage blow with his sword. "And reward my enemies!"

Even the hardened searats moaned in horror as the head of Bludrigg thudded to the floor. The coronet rolled in front of Gabool. He picked it up on the dripping sword blade and held it forth to the assembly.

"Would anyone else like to wear the crown, mateys?"

•   •   •

Heralded by the call of seabirds, eastern sunrays flooded warm and golden into a sky of calm blue reflected in the millpond sea below. The angry storm had passed, leaving summer serenity in its wake. The sun warmed the wet bundle on the flotsam-strewn tideline until it stirred. Seawater and bile flooded from the mousemaid's mouth as she coughed feebly. The damp paw set tiny flies buzzing as it reached for her throat and began weakly grappling with the knotted rope. The wooden spar lay across her back. A seabird landed upon it; the added weight caused the mousemaid to vomit more salt water forth with a gurgling groan. Startled, the bird rose noisily into the air, cheated of the carcass it had taken for dead. Other seabirds began to wheel and circle overhead. A tiny crab tried nibbling at the maid's rough wet burlap dress, gave up and scuttled away.

Finally undone, the rope fell away from her bruised neck. Painfully she shifted the spar and rolled over onto her back. The mousemaid lay still awhile; some of the more venturesome seabirds spiraled lower. Rubbing sand and grit from her face with the back of a paw, she opened both eyes, immediately shutting them again against the glare of sunlight. Small wavelets trickled and lapped gently away from the shore; the tide was ebbing. The mousemaid ventured to explore the wound that the spar had inflicted upon her head. She winced and left it alone. Turning over again, she shielded her eyes with her paws and rested on the firm damp sand, soaking up the lifegiving rays of the comforting sun. A large speckled gull landed close to her. Readying its dangerous beak, it stalked slowly forward; the mousemaid watched it from between her paws. Within a neck-length of her prostrate body the sea gull stood upon one webbed foot and began bringing its beak down in an exploratory peck.

Thwack!

She swung the wet-sand-weighted end of the rope. It was knotted and her aim was good. The rope's end thudded solidly into the bird's right eye. With a squawk of pain and distress the sea gull did an awkward running takeoff, flopping into the air and dispersing its alarmed companions.

The little mousemaid began dragging herself laboriously up the beach, her throat parched, mouth dry, head aching, limbs battered almost numb by the pounding seas. She reached a tussock of reedgrass in the dry sand above the tideline. Pulling the grass about her, she lay down in the safety of its shelter. As sleep descended upon her weary body, strange thoughts flooded her mind. She could not remember who she was, she had no name she could recall; apart from the stormy seas that had tossed her up, there was no memory of anything—it was all a cloudy gray void. Where had she come from? Where was she now? What was she doing here? Where was she going? Her last thought before sleep enveloped her brain was that she was a fighter. She could beat off a large sea gull with a rope's end, even lying stranded and half-dead from exhaustion, and she had survived the sea.

She was alive! . . .

5

The midday sun glinted off the waters of the far northwest sea as thick-headed revelers from the previous night hauled anchors to sail out and scour the seas or range the coasts in their constant search for plunder and booty, slaves and trinkets. Gabool the Wild watched them from the high window of his banqueting hall, *Waveblade*, *Blacksail*, *Rathelm* and *Greenfang*, four good craft laden with the rakings and scrapings of seas and oceans, murderers all.

Gabool had conferred captaincy of the *Greenfang* on Garrtail, an up-and-coming member of the searat brethren, but dull and wholly servile to his master Gabool, Lord of all Waters. Dull Garrtail might be, but Gabool knew that it would not stop him gossiping to the master of the *Darkqueen*, Saltar, brother of Bludrigg. Garrtail knew that the *Darkqueen* habitually ranged the seas to the south; he would make sure his path crossed with Saltar. There was little doubt the corsair master of *Darkqueen* would hear the tale of his brother's death, chapter and verse.

Gabool tore at a leg of roasted kittiwake and chewed

reflectively. Saltar had the reputation of being a hard searat to cross. Though they had never matched blades, Gabool knew Saltar to be a corsair hook fighter, using a vicious metal hook to impale opponents before slaying them with his curved sword. Gabool spat the meat away and hurled the kittiwake leg out of the window, watching it bounce off rocks on the sheer face until it hit the sea below.

He laughed slyly. Two could play at that game!

Taking a long dagger from his waist sash, Gabool went to the far end of the hall. A colored cloth wall hanging, held outward by a wooden rail near the ceiling, reached from on high down to the floor. Gabool pushed it to one side and found the crack in the stonework behind it. He jammed the long dagger, handle first, into the crack so that it was wedged, with the blade pointing outward, then let the wall hanging fall back into place. Though he was a renowned fighter and a fearless one, Gabool never took chances, particularly since the incident with the mouse-maid. Standing back, Gabool surveyed the trap. Good, the wall hanging looked like any other in the hall, perfectly harmless.

Now his restless eye was caught by the great bell. He wandered around its wide perimeter, fascinated by the object. Surely no Searat King had ever taken such a magnificent prize. Gabool pinged it with his long curving claws, sounded it by banging his rings and bracelets upon its brazen surface, amazed by the clear musical noises it made, tingling, humming and vibrating. He bared his lips. Leaning close in, he bit lightly at it, making his gold teeth reverberate with the echoes from the bell. Gabool stroked the cool curving object as he crooned softly.

"Speak to me, beauty, we must get to know each other well. I am Gabool the Wild, your owner, but you need not fear me. Your voice will call to my feet one day, your tones will terrify my enemies. You will be the voice of Gabool when I set you atop of my fort and let your tongue swing free. Then, ah then, you will boom out across the waves so that all the seas will know Gabool is King."

On a sudden impulse Gabool dashed off. Slamming the door behind him, he took the downward stairs three at a time, deeper and deeper into the depths of his own lair. Two guards were standing at the entrance to the prison cells. Gabool whirled upon them with a snarl.

"Get out of my sight and leave me alone here!"

As the guards fled, Gabool made his way to a cell that was little more than a cage. He lounged against the bars, grinning at the pitiful creature locked up inside.

"Well, bellmaker, ready to work for me yet?"

Joseph the Bellmaker was chained by his waist to the wall. The floor of the subterranean cell was awash with sea water which seeped through from outside. Joseph had once been a powerful, well-fleshed mouse, but now his cheeks were sunken and dark circles formed around his eyes. Starvation and ill treatment had taken their ruthless toll on the bellmaker, though as he raised his head, both eyes burned with remorseless hatred for his captor.

"I would sooner be eaten by the fishes of the sea than serve you, rat."

Gabool continued as if he had not heard the prisoner. "You can do it, Joseph, I know you can. A bell tower strong enough to hold the great bell, right on top of my fort, where the whole world will hear it."

Joseph pulled forward, straining at the chain in the enclosed space, his voice shaking with pent-up rage.

"Never. I would not soil my paws with your mad ideas and evil schemes. That bell was made for the badger, the Lord of Salamandastron, enemy of all sea-scum. It will never ring for you!"

Gabool drew his sword and clashed it against the cell bars.

"Hell's guts! D'you think I care who it was made for, you fool? The bell is mine now, mine to do what I like with. Its voice will sound for me alone. I, Gabool, War-lord of the Waves, say this!"

Joseph slumped down, shaking his head in despair.

"You're mad, completely insane and evil. Kill me, do what you want with me, I don't care anymore."

Gabool sheathed his sword. Drawing close to the bars he whispered low, "And your daughter?"

The bellmaker's face betrayed the agony his mind was suffering.

"No, please! You wouldn't harm her, you couldn't! She's so young and, and. . . . Don't you dare hurt my daughter!"

Gabool now sorely regretted drowning the bellmaker's daughter. Still, if the old buffoon thought she was alive, there might be a bit of fun here. Gabool decided to toy with his victim.

"If you build my bell tower I will let you see her again, but not until you've carried out the work."

Joseph tugged at the chain. He bit his lip until blood showed, torn by the decision he knew he had to make.

"Gabool, listen. I would not put a single stone atop another for you. Why? Because it would mean death, torture or slavery for countless other good creatures. Don't you understand, rat, my conscience would not let me, after I saw what they did to the Captain and crew of our ship when searats captured us. I know it means that I may never see my young one again. It tears my heart apart, but I must do the right thing for the sake of others."

Gabool summoned up all his cunning, his black soul driving him on to wickedness, belying the smile on his face as he threw his claws wide.

"Haharr, very stubborn, Joseph, but I can see that you're a good creature. Sometimes I wish that I'd never been born wicked, but decent like you. I suppose I'll have to think of somethin' else now. But hark, bellmaker, I'm sure you'd like to see your daughter again, wouldn't you, matey?"

Tears of gratitude beaded in the unsuspecting prisoner's eyes. "She means more to me than anything. Please let me see her!"

Gabool took the keys from a wallspike. "Hell's gates! I must be getting soft in me old age. Come on, then."

They stood in the banqueting hall, barbarian and bell-maker. Joseph looked around him, dragging his chains as he did.

"Where is she?"

Gabool touched the great bell with his sword. "Not so fast, shipmate. If you won't build me a bell tower, then at least tell me what these little pictures and strange words round the top 'n' bottom of my bell mean."

Joseph shuffled anxiously around the bell, his mind preoccupied with thoughts of his daughter as he reluctantly read off the rhyme at its base.

"I will ring for wedding times, when two hearts
    unite.
I will toll the hours out, all daytime and through
    night.
I will wake good creatures up, from their beds each
    morning,
Or toll when they're in danger, a clear and brazen
    warning.
For all the family, son and daughter, husband and
    goodwife,
I will boom a sad farewell, when they must leave
    this life.
For many great occasions, for many different
    reasons,
Listen and my voice you'll hear, throughout the
    changing seasons.
Though I may boom, clang, peal or toll, command
    and use me well.
But hark, beware the evil ones who would misuse
    the bell."

Gabool stared hard at Joseph. "Trash! I'll have it filed off one day. What about the little drawin's an' pictures round the top, what do they mean, bellmaker?"

Joseph spread his shackled paws. "Only the Lord of Salamandastron knows that. He gave me a parchment with those drawn upon it. Who knows what goes through

the minds of the great badger rulers of the fire mountain;
they are creatures of destiny. I've told you all I know,
now can I see my daughter?"

Gabool led him to the open window.

"Of course, matey, I can't show you the exact spot
where she lies, but I can show you how to find her . . ."

For Gabool it was but the work of a moment, one swift
push!

In the late afternoon the mousemaid cast a long shadow
as she wandered the deserted beach alone. Hunger, thirst
and attacks of myriad gnats and sandflies had wakened
and forced her to desert the hiding place. Over one shoulder she still carried the knotted rope. A long line of paw-
prints in the sand behind her emphasized the desolation
of sea, sand and sky, seemingly inhabited only by predatory seabirds. She had tried gnawing at some young seaweed washed up on the tideline, but the heavy salt taste
in the maiden's dry swollen mouth caused her to spit it
away. Swaying slightly, she shielded her eyes from the
hot orb of the sun and gazed about. Fresh water was
nowhere to be had. Turning inland, she made her weary
way toward a large outcrop of sand dunes to the south.

Some perverse dogged spirit drove the mousemaid on-
ward, though often she would be toppled over by the hot
shifting sand of the dunes. Rolling downhill, she would
pick herself up, wipe grit from her eyes and begin climbing again. It was on top of one difficult dune she en-
countered the first sign of life that was not a seabird. It
was a small lizard, eyes half-closed, basking in the heat.
The reptile did a sideways shuffle, watching her warily.
The maiden tried several times to communicate, manag-
ing only a croaking noise. The lizard's head weaved from
side to side as it snapped bad-temperedly at her.

"You norra frog, you make frognoise, wharra you
want?"

The mousemaid managed to gasp out a single word:
"Water."

The small lizard moved its head up and down, its throat pulsating.

"Water faraway. You norra lizard, you die soon, never make it to drinkwater, too far. Soon now they eat you."

She followed the creature's upward nod. Gulls were beginning to circle overhead; the scavengers of the shore, sensing when a living thing was becoming weaker and more defenseless. The maid grasped the knotted rope and swung it, calling at the sky in a hoarse voice, "I'm not finished yet. You'll see!"

When she looked down, the lizard had gone. Without a backward glance she descended the other side of the dune, half stumbling, half falling. The foot of the dune was in shadow. Before her lay a sandy flatland dotted with scrub and coarse grass. The little mousemaid rested awhile in the welcoming shade. Idly her paw sank into the sand as she leaned back. Suddenly she sat bolt upright. The sand was firm and damp just beneath the surface. Realization that she was not on the seaward side of the dunes brought with it the shining hope of one precious thing. Water!

Scrabbling dizzily, her strength failing rapidly, the maid began digging with all paws. Soon she was rewarded by darker, damp sand. Her paws made a delicious scraping noise as she tossed sand out of the shallow hole. Digging with the urgency of desperation, she was finally rewarded with one wet paw. She sat sucking her paw as the moisture seeped through the ground into the hole, forming a small muddy pool. Throwing herself flat, the little mousemaid shoved her head into the hole and drank greedily, disregarding the gritty sand and ooze, as life-giving water flowed down her throat. New vitality surged through her. Gurgling with delight, she lifted her head and found herself staring into the predatory eye of a gannet that had been sneaking up on her.

Thwack! Thwop!

With eye-blurring speed she belted the knotted rope twice into the bird's face. It stumbled, fell over, sticklike legs buckling under it. The mousemaid advanced, swinging her weapon, with battle light in her eyes and a clear angry voice.

"Come on! What d'you want, the water or me? Come on. I'll fight you, you great featherbed!"

The twirling knot struck the gannet a further three times before it managed to flop off into the air with a half-stunned squawk. The little mousemaid felt the blood thrumming in her veins. She tore up a nearby plant and shook it at the sky.

"That goes for all of you. I'll kill the next one that comes after me. D'you hear?"

She found herself shouting at an empty evening sky. The birds had gone in search of less ferocious prey. Inspecting the plant she had pulled from the ground, she noticed that the root was attached to a fat white tuber. Without further hesitation she began munching upon it. The tuber tasted good, something like raw turnip.

Evening gave way to night as the maid sat at the foot of the dune, bathing the wound on her head with a corner of her burlap smock which she had soaked in water from her newfound well. Dabbing at the cut with one paw and devouring a root held in the other, the mousemaid talked aloud to herself, enjoying the sound of her own voice.

"No name, no memory, no idea where I am. Ha! I know, I'll call myself Storm, because it was the storm that brought me here. Yes, Storm, I like that . . ."

She held the rope up and twirled it. "And you are my faithful Gullwhacker. There, we've both got new names now. This is good—I've got you, the shade from my sandhill, water and food."

Storm settled down in the sand as the warm summer night closed in on her. "Wish I knew who I really was, though . . ." Her voice sounded small and lonely amid the scrub and desolation.

A pale golden moon peeped over the dunes at the little mousemaid sleeping by the foot of the hill, clutching a piece of knotted rope, for all the world like some infant in slumber nursing a favorite toy.